T5-CRO-667

BUCK

Also by Bill Burchardt

THE BIRTH OF LOGAN STATION
SHOTGUN BOTTOM
YANKEE LONGSTRAW
THE MEXICAN

BUCK

BILL BURCHARDT

DOUBLEDAY & COMPANY, INC.

GARDEN CITY, NEW YORK

1978

All of the characters in this book are fictitious, and any resemblance
to actual persons, living or dead, is purely coincidental.

ISBN: 0-385-13439-8
Library of Congress Catalog Card Number 78-1188

BUCK

I

Buck Mather watched the shadowy silhouette of the Ford touring car parked in the night darkness ahead of him. He pedaled his own T-Model into low gear, and proceeded down the dirt road with clandestine deliberation.

He knew where he was. He was in the big hollow just this side of Cimarron Bend. It was up this same draw that he and Bud had tortuously worked their way one bitterly cold morning last February seeking Jabe Vandergriff's whiskey still.

The dim yellow cones from the headlights of Buck's car crept patiently up the narrow dirt road before him, approaching the hazy outline of the touring car which sat pulled off into one track of this rough back-country road, its right wheels sloping off down into the weedy dark of the barrow ditch.

It could be the robbery vehicle. Buck could make out the distinctive shape of the Ford's black waterproof top, hazy in the shadows of the low, slowly rising, summer moon. Even over the well-tuned clatter of his own motor, he could hear the insect din and tree-frog racket that pervaded the hollow here where Skeleton Creek ran off toward the Cimarron.

Though the headlights had not quite reached it, and the parked car ahead seemed deserted, Buck sensed that it was not. No hurry. Calm patience was the way. Give the other fellow's nerves time to jangle, let his heart race. Buck inhaled deeply of the moist summer night air, redolent with the odor of damp decay here in the hollow.

His headlights reached the touring car's rear tires, crept

on up over its fenders, then the yellow isinglass of its back window, and along the side of the motionless vehicle. Still no sign of human occupancy. The seats were empty.

Then Buck saw the man. He was standing in front of the touring car's radiator. Buck pulled up alongside, threw his motor into idle and called out cheerfully, "Having trouble?"

"Not me," the man answered peevishly, "but this damn radiator—"

Buck switched off his headlights, stepped over the dummy door on the driver's side, and walked unhurriedly around the front of his own car. In the shifting dark of shadows moving gently in the night wind, the man had been standing relieving himself. He was bent slightly forward now buttoning up his pants and as Buck approached he finished the buttoning and in smooth hand motion swept aside his coattails.

Buck recognized the motion and stepped in close to confront him. As the man drew the gun concealed behind his hip, Buck slid his own .45 from its leather holster. The man leveled his gun on Buck's belly and Buck reached to slip his forefinger behind the trigger of his opponent's gun. No use killing a man needlessly.

But now things got slightly complicated. The man Buck confronted did exactly the same thing. He had slipped his forefinger behind the trigger of Buck's gun. No nervousness here. Buck Mather's quarry this time was as cold nerved as he was. They stood there deadlocked.

As extra insurance Buck eased the web of flesh between his thumb and forefinger down between the cocked hammer and cartridge of his opponent's weapon. The shallow breathing gent before him followed suit. If either had succeeded in pulling a trigger the hammer would have fallen only to pinch live flesh rather than to explode the cartridge it was purposed to fire.

Neither said anything in the tension of the deadlock. The engine in Buck's Ford hoopy coughed and died. The new silence was sudden and utter, even quieting the insect noise and the croaking of the tree frogs. Then Bud Reed's voice came hotly out of the dark behind the man Buck had sought to take without gunfire.

"All right, mister!" Deputy Reed's voice was taut with excitement. "Turn loose of the pistol butt, and let the sheriff have your gun! Easy now!"

The man's dark eyes sparkled angrily at Buck. "Sheriff? Is that who you are?" He swung his head around to address the roadside dark behind him, "Where in the hell did *you* come from?"

"Buck dropped me off about fifty yards back down the road when he slowed to come up on your car." Deputy Bud Reed's voice was still tight and ready as he came up out of the bar ditch weeds to prod his victim's back with his revolver barrel.

"Well, hell, it's a standoff," declared the man.

"It sure as the devil is," Bud challenged. "You kill Buck and I'll blow a hole in your back big enough to stick my fist into."

"What do you fellows want with me?" the man demanded.

He released his gun and Buck took it.

"Well, the ticket window at the Odeon Vaudeville was robbed about forty-five minutes ago, during the picture show," Buck said mildly. "I expect the cashier will recognize you. She said the gent who held her up got in a Ford touring car at the curb and drove off. What happened to your car?"

"The damned thing boiled over!"

"Where were you headed?" Bud grilled him.

"None of your business."

Buck figured it was an unnecessary question. Cimarron Bend and its oilrush boomtown were less than four miles further down the road. Bud was rummaging around in the dark tonneau of the touring car.

"There's a cloth sack full of money, mostly silver, in here, Buck," Bud called out.

"Bring it back," Buck said. With the man's .38 caliber Smith & Wesson in the palm of his big left hand, Buck motioned toward his car with his own .45 Colt. "Get in."

The man moved, reluctantly.

"What'll we do with his machine?" Bud asked.

The touring car's radiator was still gurgling ominously in fitful, subdued boiling. "Let it set here till morning," Buck replied. "It'll cool off by then. We can send Sparky out to fill up the radiator and drive it in." He stepped to follow his prisoner.

"You're new around here, aren't you?" Buck asked. "What's your name?"

The suspect retorted peevishly, "I'll tell you when I'm damn good and ready!"

"That'll be fine," Buck replied mildly. He paused to watch the man crawl into his T-Model's front seat.

Buck walked around to step over the door on the driver's side. He set the throttle and the spark, and waited while Bud did the cranking. With the motor running, Bud ran to get in on the left side, and Buck shoved down the reverse pedal.

The forty-five-minute drive back to Logan Station was accomplished for the most part without talking. Buck knew that his young deputy, of unquestioned courage, had a short attention span and he didn't want to distract him. Let Bud concentrate on the unknown quantity riding in the seat between them.

Besides, Buck knew he had not been driving this newfangled Ford long enough to get overconfident. It wasn't like his big stud horse Chalky, who was dependable. This critter seemed to have a contrary mind of its own and Buck knew from experience it could cut off across the ruts for the barbwire fence, its steering wheel as hard to hang on to as a jumping bull calf by a branding fire.

The silent hombre in the middle of the close-crowded car seat was like a tight strung strand of that barbwire, too. Buck was not likely to forget his own slight surprise at the aplomb of this captive whose dexterous finger had slid through his trigger guard behind Buck's own finger with such smooth co-ordination, tying Buck's move with an exactness that could not have improved with any amount of practice.

A wrong move here, let Bud Reed get a little distracted, let the Ford perform just a hair erratically, or, Sheriff Buck Mather told himself, let his own attention wander, and this chilly nerved customer they'd taken prisoner could go "spang" like that overtight barbwire. Primed and ready, he'd have his own gun back, or one of theirs, and it could turn into a bloody Saturday night.

Bud passed a comment on the number of teams still hauling freight, or returning empty from the oilfield, in spite of the late hour of the night, as they turned into the main road to Logan Station. Buck grunted in noncommittal agreement, and kept on driving. They pulled in past the water tower at the west end of town, turned into Broad Street, rumbling over cobblestone brick paving alongside the streetcar tracks as they approached the center of town. They passed the darkened office of Logan Station's daily newspaper. Buck pulled up to stop two doors down, beside the bicycle rack in front of the Odeon.

"Get out," he told the prisoner.

Taking a firm grip on the man's right arm, Buck led him to the ticket wicket. "Is this him, Susie?" he asked.

The chubby, pretty picture show cashier strained forward to look out into the gaslight glow spilling from her ticket booth.

"That's him, Mr. Mather," she agreed.

As they pulled away from the Odeon, a lonely figure in

the center of the intersection at the edge of the courthouse square caught their attention.

Bud said, "Oh-oh. John Barnhouse is at it again."

They approached the square, where the county courthouse stood in Victorian splendor, and the rough garbed man in the intersection motioned them over to the curb. Buck pulled up and stopped.

Barnhouse, wearing a policeman's hat, a metal star, and carrying a toy billy club came to lean and peer cautiously at the three faces inside the car. He was a tall raw-boned man, rough hewn and awkwardly jointed, who looked as if he would be more comfortable swinging an axe. Recognizing Buck, John Barnhouse said, "Oh. It's you, Chief." His toy billy club rattled against the side of the car as he lifted his hand in mock salute. His policeman's cap was too small, obviously a phony of the cheap racket-store variety, perched atop his ragged, uncut hair.

Buck said, "Good evening, John. Everything quiet?"

The metal badge, a star stamped out of tin and pinned to Barnhouse's blue work shirt, was part of the same set, star, billy club and cap attached to a cardboard and purchasable at the toy counter of the local racket store.

"Yessir, Chief," Barnhouse assured the sheriff. "Everything quiet. Real quiet. I haven't made an arrest all evening."

"Very well, John." Buck nodded soberly. "Carry on."

He eased the Ford into low gear and as they drove away from the curb, the addle-witted Barnhouse returned to his lonely station in the center of the intersection to continue directing nonexistent traffic.

Bud groused, "We ought to lock that looney up, Buck!"

Buck made no reply. He drove on around to the rear of the courthouse and into the wagon yard. Here he parked in sight of the jail entrance, nodded at the prisoner, and said, "Take him in, Bud."

Buck then sat behind the steering wheel eying the area

watchfully. It was a long hundred yards from the Ford to the jail entrance, mellowly flooded now with the light of a well risen moon. Buck watched the shadowy pair approach the jail doorway, his eyes moving carefully from Bud and his prisoner to every other shadow in the wagon yard—the clump he knew to be the road crew's chuck wagon with the fresnos and dragline moldboards which surrounded it, the darkly standing bulk of the wellhouse nearby, and the slender structure of the jail outhouse which stood farther back and separated from all other outbuildings.

But nothing moved except Bud and the prisoner. Buck saw Bud lean to pick up something from the ground, then he heard the jangle of his deputy's keys unlocking the jailhouse door. Buck saw the door swing open. He got out of the car.

By the time Buck had crossed the open space to gain entrance to the courthouse, Bud had already locked the prisoner up and returned to the sheriff's office. He was standing beside Buck's desk unfolding tomorrow's Sunday morning paper, picked up in the jail doorway. As Buck made his way around the desk to his own swivel chair he caught the pleasant savor of fresh newsprint and printer's ink from the newly printed edition.

Bud tossed the front page news section to Buck and stood concentrating on the full page ad for the Hagenbeck Circus, scheduled to show Sunday matinee and evening at the Logan Station Livestock Exposition grounds. Buck observed the almost boyish play of emotions crossing his young deputy's dark, almost swarthy face as Bud scanned the center display of a hugely maned lion leaping through a flaming hoop and read the banner of 100-PERFORMERS-100, in second coming sized type, easily readable from where Buck sat.

Lion tamers and trapeze performers manifestly held more fascination for young Bud than the latest violence and tragedies perpetrated in the county's Cimarron Bend oilfield, which always dominated the Logan Station *Leader*'s front page. Neither did Buck find any pleasure in their grimness.

He turned to the editorial page, and was even less entertained by what he encountered there. A cartooned dummy, labeled Logan Station, was being lynched by a horde of grimacing devils, individually labeled *crime, robbery, booze, gambling, prostitution, licentiousness, evil, outrage, vexation, sin,* and on and on. Buck laid the newspaper down on his desk rather forcefully.

"I guess we'll have to book him 'John Doe,'" he said.

Bud, reluctantly, tore his eyes away from the circus advertisement. "Huh?" he asked.

"Our prisoner," Buck reminded him patiently. "That malefactor you just locked up back there."

"Oh." The stars faded in Bud's eyes as he gradually brought them back in focus on the present. "That's Wiley Lester," he said. "I recognized him as soon as I saw him in good light here in the office."

Buck felt a little of his patience drain away. "You know that scissorbill?"

"Yeah." Bud's gaze was headed for the circus ad again.

"Why didn't you say so?"

"You didn't ask me." Bud Reed looked pained and a little nettled at these steady interruptions. "He's been hanging around Cimarron Bend for a while. I seen him playing cards in Barney Arles' Casino about a week ago and asked who he was."

"You heard of him before?"

"Nope. He just looked like kind of bad medicine," Bud speculated. "I'm surprised he'd get caught making a poky heist on a picture show. He looked like a ring-tailed roarer to me. Maybe he'd been drinking."

Buck remembered Lester's cool mien, and the steady grip that had held his gun hand. "I don't think so. Likely he was just trying for a stake to gamble with. Any wanted bulletins on him?"

"None I've seen."

Buck's gaze was again magnetically drawn down to the cartoon on the page spread out on his desk top, and he began to read the blackly boxed editorial beneath it.

". . . *the evils of Cimarron Bend will inevitably contaminate the life of Logan Station,*" the editorial contended. "*To our certain knowledge, such notorious characters as Etta Redmond, proprietress of that oilrush house of ill fame called The Green Tree, Isaac Price, whose saloon is known as The Same Old Ikey's, and Barney Arles, owner of the infamous Casino, have all bought homes in our fair city.*

"*They live here, although they work (if it can be called that) fourteen miles away in Cimarron Bend. Their presence in Logan Station cannot be other than a harbinger of worse to come.*"

Buck inserted the editorial between the full page spread about the circus and Bud's fixed gaze. His young deputy read the boldface tirade, exploded profanely, and flung the newspaper down. As it fell, it flapped shut to again expose its front page. The headline of a feature story set in the lower left corner caught Bud's eye and he snatched it up anew.

He read silently for a moment, then began reading aloud. "'*Sheriff Mather and Deputy Reed,*'" he quoted the article, "'*are rarely seen walking together. Rather, the sheriff will proceed well out in advance, with his deputy following along thirty or forty yards to the rear.*'

"'*In this way,*'" Bud glanced meaningfully at his boss, "'*any miscreant so ill advised as to attack our sheriff soon finds himself double-teamed from the rear*'—Damn it Buck! They've give away our M.O.—the way we work!"

Buck was less perturbed. "It would have, I reckon, if hooligans could read. Which they sometimes can, but seldom do. No cause to boil over," Buck calmed him.

"'Since Sheriff Mather and Deputy Reed are seldom seen together,'" Bud read on, "'the hapless evildoer must forever feel unsafe, even fearful, when either of them is encountered alone. For the other officer is likely to be lurking nearby. Logan Station's civic leaders, in the forefront of the swelling demand for regulation of Cimarron Bend's wickedness, place great hope in the effectiveness of Buck Mather and Bud Reed.'

"'The Reverend Mark Jellico has been quoted as saying, "Like sinful Gomorrah, Cimarron Bend should be wiped from the face of the earth!" Redoubtable Judge Caleb Hull, strong right arm of the law, states, "Unless there is prompt betterment in the disgraceful and shameful situation of lawlessness which exists in the oilfield"'—crap!" Bud Reed ripped out the expletive, unrestrained in his wrath, and flung the newspaper at the rifle rack.

Its pages fluttered apart en route, scattering wildly. Bud savagely flung himself into the office chair opposite Buck's desk. Pettish and sullen, he muttered, "That pair of pusillanimous prigs!"

"It's serious," Buck agreed. "Cimarron Bend wants no law enforcement at all. The blue noses here in Logan Station want too much. How do you walk a chalk line like that?"

Buck paused reflectively. "That Cowboy Flat country out there in the big bend of the Cimarron has been breeding outlaws ever since Ben and Oscar Hazlitt ranched there in the early days, hiring the likes of the Dalton Brothers, Bill Doolin, and Bittercreek Newcomb. When Doolin quit cowboying and put together his gang, Cimarron Bend was the place they went to hole up, to blow in their money and celebrate after every robbery."

Bud Reed had calmed down some, but he still fumed. "Since the oil discovery the town is full of lonesome men without families who don't give a damn. They just want to raise hell themselves. They've got no women folks or kids to

look after. There ain't a school or a church in the town!"
Both men sat silently.

The lateness of the night's hour seemed to filter into the
quiet office, weighing impressively. From the cell area beyond the partition, Buck could hear old man Foley, the
night jailer, whistling tunelessly. Buck got up.

"Good night, Bud," he said. "It's away past time for me to
go home to my wife."

His deputy sat, pouting sullenly. Bud said peevishly, "I
think I'll go down to the railroad spur at the Livestock Exposition grounds and watch the circus set up."

II

Buck undressed in fumbling silence in the musky quiet of the bedroom. His wife, Kaahtidoah, was sleeping, breathing deeply. The moonlight fell mysteriously across her elegant, mature features, heightening their rich mixture of Kiowa-Mexican handsomeness.

Buck smiled, thinking it was no wonder those Kiowa Indian boys had kept making up war parties year after year to raid south in Mexico and steal themselves a wife. What a combination those bloodlines had wrought in Kaahtidoah—the doll-like prettiness of Spanish beauty combined with high cheekboned Kiowa strength. The shape of her full breasted, hourglass figure showed plainly through the light coverlet she had pulled up to shield her, for the humid coolness of the moist summer night often turned to a slight morning chill as the late after-midnight hours wore away.

Prior to meeting Kaahtidoah, Buck had been a lifelong bachelor. He had first encountered her at a Kiowa O-ho-ma ceremonial near Anadarko where Buck had gone to pick up a renegade. Buck was then forty—Kaahtidoah had been twenty-three. Her grandfather, the old Chief Konandoah, and Buck had taken a prompt liking for each other. Kaahtidoah's own father had died of alcoholism when she was just a little girl.

Konandoah served the Kiowa people in a manner somewhat similar to a Supreme Court justice. Those who had disputes brought their problems to him. He listened, and rendered a decision, judgments the Kiowas always meticulously followed. Buck and Konandoah had spent many hours in each other's company, mostly, in the old Indian way, in silence—communicating in the spirit rather than with spoken words.

When the time had come for Buck to ask for Kaahtidoah's hand in marriage, that too had been surprisingly like the old ways of more than a generation past. Except that Buck had provided a feast of barbecued beef instead of buffalo for his Kiowa friends and, instead of making the old chief a gift of horses, had given Konandoah a fine pair of carefully fitted spectacles, to restore his eyesight in return for his granddaughter's hand in marriage.

After five years of pleasant and lively marriage to Buck, Kaahtidoah now twenty-eight and Buck forty-five, his only real concern regarding her was that he might become an impotent old man before she lost her desire. As he looked at her at this moment, sleeping there in the moonlight, that did not seem to be an imminent danger.

She stirred as Buck's fumbling fingers dropped one of his boots and it made a clunk on the floor. So slightly aroused, her eyes fluttered open. She said nothing, but smiled, warmly and sleepily. Buck chucked the other boot under the bed and lifted the coverlet.

It was nearly noon when he awakened. Kaahtidoah, awake but quiescent, still rested beside him. It was another hour before they arose to breakfast on crisply fried pork chops, biscuits and gravy, while consuming two successive pots of strong black coffee. Afterward he walked out to the horse barn to look at the Ford, standing in the center runway of the weathered, board floored, hay smelling stable.

Shafts of dusty sunlight sifted down through wide cracks between the old barn's dry boards to display, in their latticework of light, the car, and the sheriff's horse. Chalky, a powerhouse of horse nearly seventeen hands high, bright white in color, seemed almost to reflect the sunlight back upward toward its source. The stallion stood hipshot, quietly munching alfalfa hay grown and cured in the rich redbed bottomlands across the same Cimarron which, in its big bend, harbored the oilrush boomtown that now dominated Buck's thoughts and life, and gave the pious and righteous residents of county seat Logan Station recurring nightmares.

Buck debated briefly between the automobile and the horse, and chose Chalky. He saddled and bridled the stallion, then stepped across to settle himself in the smoothly polished kack of hand tooled and engraved leather, and rode out into the somnolent early Sunday afternoon.

He reined out of the comfortably middle-class residence area in which he and Kaahtidoah lived, and turned toward town at the site where the new Carnegie Library was under construction. He had seen the architect's drawings and it would be, on a small scale, a magnificent structure of yellow brick and golden sandstone. Broad stairs ascending grandly to a portico supported by Doric columns, though Victorian over-all, with a graceful central dome to dominate its place against the sky.

Chalky climbed on up the gentle slope of Logan Avenue, his walking hoofs echoing on the cobblestone brick paving. In the serene quiet of the Sunday afternoon Chalky's iron shod hoofs seemed especially noisy. The big stallion had begun to sweat a little and the strong, horsy odor of him rose pleasantly to Buck's nostrils, serving to further elevate the sheriff's good humor.

Had it been a normal business day, he would have been steadily occupied saluting friends and acquaintances, with a lifted hand, a point of a finger, a smile, a wave, a touch of the hat brim to the ladies—there were few people in Logan Station Buck Mather did not know, and even fewer who did not know him.

But it was Sunday and Logan Station's "blue law" was full in effect. Business houses were closed. The streets were deserted, and the popular county sheriff rode in lonely and majestic silence.

Feeling a little resentment toward a "blue law" so severely enforced that it emptied the streets of the town of
people, leaving virtually no place to go but the interminably
long church services held morning and night in a dozen
churches of different denominations in the town, Buck rode
past Garland's Cigar Factory, and the small lunch-wagon
eatery across the street, both tightly closed.

Another block and he was in the town's main business
section, empty and deserted except, of course, for The Owl
Drug Store, which was open to provide patent medicines,
nostrums, and prescriptions for the sick. The Owl Drug had
a soda fountain, surrounded by a few marble topped tables
and their twisted wire chairs. The drug store sold news-
papers, magazines, and a variety of ladies' cosmetics and
sundries.

So it was a bright spot of activity on these silent Sundays.
Two autos were parked before it, their empty seats reflect-
ing the glint of the afternoon sun from shiny leather uphol-
stery. Doc Bell's carriage, a spanking new buggy, stood at
the curb. Doc's chestnut gelding was harnessed in the traces
and tied to the half-round iron weight Doc had dropped in
the street beside the gelding's left front hoof.

The Floradora Pool Hall next door was closed up tight,
which started Buck wondering why the city fathers had let
the circus show on a Sunday? Greed, he guessed. Better
than on a business day, especially a Saturday. The circus
would have brought a crowd into town, but the stores of the
penurious merchants would have stood empty for hours
while everyone went to the circus.

At the Gray Brothers' Bank corner, Buck turned off to circle the town square, rode through a block containing two
closed grocery stores, a hardware, a realty-abstract office,
Rushing's ice cream manufacturing plant, and Talmadge's
sprawling livery barn—all locked and silent—and pulled
Chalky up at the metal hitching post reserved for the sheriff

in front of the big ugly county building which housed his office and the jail.

He left the stallion to enjoy the salubrious and balmy air. A light breeze blew and ruffled Chalky's white mane, tossing it in flowing horse riffles. The horse stood in the shade of the great elm that spread its branches over the hitching post. Buck walked to his office's front entrance and went inside, to almost instant abandonment of the serenity with which he had started the day.

Day jailer Shorty Long, hearing the sheriff enter, cracked open the door to the cell block to thrust his homely round face into the sheriff's office and report, "You had a telephone call from the right reverend Mark Jellico about half an hour ago, Buck."

Buck thanked him and, while peeling off his kidskin riding gloves, asked Shorty to get in touch with Logan Station's mechanic, Sparky North. He told Shorty where Sparky would find Wiley Lester's car abandoned, and to arrange with the mechanic to bring it into town. Then Buck went directly to the wall telephone.

He rang central. "Laura?"

"Good afternoon, Sheriff," the telephone operator answered.

"Ring preacher Jellico at the parsonage, will you?"

Buck could tell that she was hesitant. "He'll be taking his Sunday afternoon nap, won't he?" the girl asked.

"Hate to disturb his reverence," Buck agreed, "but he called me. He's likely to be more upwrought if I don't call than if I do."

"Yes," she said, but she sounded rueful. Buck could hear the ring as she plugged in.

After talking his way past a similar reluctance on the part of the reverend's wife to awaken her resting husband, Mark Jellico's usually honeyed and unctuous voice, now more surly than pious, came cantankerously over the wire.

He informed Buck that the Logan Station ministerial alliance, of which he was chairman, had met for luncheon at the Harvey House and voted to recommend that the sheriff appoint a special oilfield deputy at once.

Buck cogitated.

"Well," he began, "I know a fellow—"

"Is he courageous?" demanded Jellico. "Have you worked with him?"

"I worked with him in Johnson County, Wyoming, a few years ago," Buck said. "In those days he'd go out of his way to get in a fight."

"That sounds promising," Jellico said brusquely. "We need a man who is unafraid to carry forth fearful judgments. He should become a resident of Cimarron Bend and be ready for action. The vengeance of God must be wrought, the guilty must be scourged, even with the use of firearms! The wages of sin is death, and the psalmist tells us that the ways of the wicked shall perish—"

The central girl interrupted the call. "Reverend Jellico, I hate to break in like this, but someone has been trying to ring through to the sheriff's office from the circus grounds. He says it is an emergency."

"What's the emergency?" Buck inquired calmly.

"The caller identified himself as the circus owner," Laura said. "According to him, the lion tamer issued a challenge to anyone in the audience to enter the cage with him and the lions. Your deputy took him up on it. He's in the lions' cage now and can't get out. It must be Bud Reed—"

Buck forgot Mark Jellico and hung up the receiver without even saying good-bye. Leaving his kidskin gloves on the desk he ran to mount Chalky and rode the less than a mile to the Exposition grounds in two minutes flat.

As he left the stallion ground tied before the big top's main entrance he could hear the rhythmic jungle roll of deep throated calliope music inside the sprawling tent.

Buck shoved past the ticket taker who tried to stop him. A brief but forceful display of the sheriff's badge beneath the

flap of his leather vest took care of that and he hurried
through the menagerie tent which prefaced entrance into
the ringed arena of the circus tent itself.

The menagerie animals, sensing that something unusual
was going on inside the big top, were pacing or running
around the inside of their ornate, wheeled cages. Monkey
squeals, the shrill trumpet of an elephant, and excited neigh-
ing along the long row of tied performing horses marked
Buck's passage. The roar of a caged and pacing tiger and
the maniac laugh of a hyena cage where the sawdust of the
arena bordered the menagerie tent did nothing to calm
Buck's perturbation as he strode into the arena.

The crowded audience was all standing. The sound they
produced was a nerve-jangling clamor hardly to be as-
sociated with anything human as they watched the drama in
the center cage. Bud was still in there all right. He had
somehow worked his way around to the opposite side of the
big round cage, where he stood with his back against its ver-
tical bars.

His left sleeve, nearest Buck, was lacerated. In the bloody
hand that protruded from it Bud held a four-legged stool he
had snatched from the circle of stools on which the lions
were supposed to perch. In his right hand was his .45, and
he fired a sudden shot into the sawdust covered earth in
front of the nose of a lion that chose that moment to charge
him.

Another of the heavy maned lions came at Bud then and
he poked the stool toward the beast. It halted to claw at the
confusing four legs thrust toward its yawning, angrily roaring jaws. The rumbling jungle music of the calliope, meant
to distract the crowd, made the wild scene seem more tu-
multuous.

Buck ran on up to the cage. The lion tamer himself was
inside, cracking his blacksnake whip viciously, occasionally
firing the small silver-plated pistol he held in a frantic at-

tempt to drive his seven huge, out-of-control performing cats back onto the pedestals they were meant to occupy.

An assistant, a roughly dressed teen-age boy with a long prod pole, ran to and fro outside the cage trying to assist the trainer. As Buck came up alongside the assistant, the youth spotted Buck's badge beneath his vest and demanded, "Get that fool smart aleck out of there!"

The calliope faltered and the circus band struck up a thunder and blazes circus march. The music totally failed to claim the crowd's attention, and Buck heard himself shouting, "Your boss invited him in!"

"Hell no he didn't!" the assistant denied. "That business is always part of the ringmaster's pitch for Signor Lucigni's act. Your deputy was standing over there by the hippodrome track like he was on crowd control duty—that's how he got in free, I reckon. Mostly he was watching the show. When the ringmaster announced that no other living human dared enter the cage with Signor Lucigni and his man-eating beasts, your deputy just came out here, unhooked the latch on the big cage, and walked in."

The assistant ran to prod back another of the lions stalking Bud. "Them cats ain't *used* to having anybody but the Signor in there with them," he yelled. "They don't know what to do!"

Any more than Bud does, Buck thought grimly.

"They smell blood now," the assistant declared, "and they're getting ferocious. They'll knock this damn jerry-built cage down into separate pieces and be loose in this crowd—"

Parents had begun streaming for the exit hurrying fearful children before them, and Buck could see spectators dropping to the ground from behind the wooden seat tiers to escape beneath the tent's side walls. Buck pulled his own gun, went to the cage entrance, and cautiously let himself in.

Backing around the periphery of the circular cage, moving warily in an effort to attract as little attention as possible from the raging cats, Buck edged around alongside Bud.

"Keep your back to the bars," he urged. "We'll start working our way back around to that door—" One of the beasts came at him and Buck powder-burned the lion's black nose. The lions' confusion was becoming pandemonium.

The wild animal smell of the frenzied lions was near overpowering. As Buck preceded Bud, side-stepping their slow way around the cage, the sheriff saw Signor Lucigni pointing feverishly. His assistant got the message. He ran to hoist the trap door exit into the barred tunnel leading to the lions' separate cages.

Other circus roustabouts manned the line of hurriedly brought up individual cages now, as Bud thrust his four-legged stool determinedly into the slavering jaws of each new charge. Buck thought, *This will last until they all decide to come at us together*. He fired twice in front of the nose of a big cat too resolute to be discouraged, and felt a small surge of hope at his sudden recollection that circus lions are fed at the conclusion of each of their performances.

One lion, hungrier than the others, or preferring a sure thing over the fighting prey on the wrong side of the cage, spotted the open tunnel to supper and scuttled out through it. The departure of the one baited the others. As a circus roustabout dropped the door to confine the exited beast with the hunk of raw meat on the floor of its own small cage, an attendant shoved the second individual cage up before the long, barred runway.

The lions poured into the runway then. Buck reached the main cage door, lifted the iron latch and hustled himself and Bud out. The audience crowding toward the main exit obviously made that way out impossible. Buck shoved Bud toward an aisle between the wooden grandstand seats. Following Bud into it, they reached the canvas side wall of the tent, lifted it, and went out into the circus back yard.

"Where's your horse?" he asked Bud.

"I'm afoot," said his deputy. "I walked down here last night after we finished talking. My horse is over in Talmadge's livery. I didn't want to go over there and saddle up and it was too late to hire a hack."

"You've been here all night?" Buck said incredulously.

"Sure! It's been interesting, Buck. You ought to watch one of these tents go up sometime. You ought to see these guys circle up to drive down stakes. They use their sledge hammers like a line of chorus girls uses their legs. Bang, bang, bang. Then the elephants go to work to stand up the center poles—"

Buck looked at the blood, still running from Bud's clawed arm. "Come on," he said, "Chalky can carry double."

The departing spectators made way for them, Bud with his arm bleeding, both of them still carrying drawn weapons. A growing crowd of pointing, babbling hangers-on formed to watch Buck mount the big white stallion, and hoist Bud up behind him.

Selecting a boy among the encircling watchers, Buck flipped him a quarter. "Son, run up to The Owl Drug Store and tell Doc Bell to come to the sheriff's house." To Bud he said, "That arm of yours is going to need some sewing up."

"I'll be all right, Buck, as soon as it quits bleeding," Bud protested.

Buck glanced at the crimson flow. "If it don't quit bleeding you're not going to have any blood left." He pulled a blue bandanna from his hip pocket. "Here, twist this around it as close as you can to your shoulder."

Bud's eyes were turning bleary. *Up all night,* Buck thought, *and now losing blood. He's not going to be able to sit this horse long.* . . . Buck turned Chalky and rode off the Exposition grounds at a fast canter.

On the way to Buck's house Bud talked of the joys of watching a circus set up, the trapeze acts rigging and testing their equipment, his speech becoming more and more slurred.

"If it hadn't of been Sunday there'd of been a parade." Bud sounded like a drunken man. "Say, ol' friend," Bud admiringly slurred, "you came in that lions' cage as calm as if you was stepping into the beanery for lunch."

Buck turned in the saddle to look back at his deputy. Bud's eyes were bleary, but a-shine with admiration.

"I figured I was stepping in there for the *lions*' lunch," Buck said. Keeping Bud talking might help keep him conscious. Buck asked, "Bud, when are you going to quit doing damn fool things?"

"Well, Buck, that ringmaster seemed so sure nobody had the guts—"

"Some things don't take guts, Bud. Sometimes common sense even takes precedence over guts, boy."

Bud threw his clawed arm across Buck's shoulder affectionately. Blood ran down Buck's leather vested shoulder and over his shirt.

Bud declared weakly, "Anyhow, boss, I sure want to thank you. I admit I done a damn fool thing—" and Deputy Bud Reed passed out as Buck reined Chalky into his own tree-shaded front yard.

Buck slid out of the saddle, hanging onto Bud to ease him down. He carried him into the house, calling out, "Kaahti—"

She had apparently seen them riding into the yard for she came bearing a basin of steaming water smelling strongly of carbolic, with washcloth and towel. Buck dumped Bud roughly onto the settee. His young deputy was tall, rangy, built of solid bone and muscle. He was almost unmanageably heavy, even for a man as broad of shoulder and strong as Buck Mather.

The sheriff untangled Bud's legs and arms, and straightened him out across the too short settee. Bud's boot shanks lay across the settee arm, keeping his feet improperly higher than his head. Kaahtidoah already had his shirt removed. She helped Buck hoist him into a half-sitting position with the settee arm beneath Bud's shoulders, and began washing and cleansing the long claw wounds with the strong smelling carbolic solution.

By the time Doc Bell arrived to inquire what had happened, and to compliment Kaahtidoah on her promptness in washing the wounds, the cleansing of them was complete. Doc brought out his sutures, sterilized them, and strung his needle.

"You've done just right, Kaahti," Doc Bell assured her. "That carbolic is strong, and there's hardly anything worse than a cat claw to cause infection. These cuts are deep."

He was a long time stitching and repairing muscle damage where the lion's claw had ripped nearly to the bone. Bud was reviving and beginning to squirm with pain before the doctor finished.

Doc shoved Bud back down when he swung his legs around and tried to sit up. "Lay there, boy! Get up and you'll fall back down. You've lost a bucket of blood."

"Is he going to be all right?" Kaahtidoah asked.

"I think so, if he'll behave himself."

"It will be all right then," Kaahti said, "if I put him to bed?"

"More than all right," declared Doc Bell. "It's going to be essential."

Kaahti Mather made ready to assist her young patient in rising.

Buck said, "If everything is under control here, I'm going to ride down to the depot. I've got a wire to send."

Doc was packing his black bag. Bud was slumped, but standing, supporting himself with an arm around Kaahti's shoulder as she eased him slowly toward the spare bedroom.

"I sure am ashamed of myself, Mrs. Mather," Bud declared dizzily.

"Feed him plenty of red meat, Kaahti," Doc Bell

suggested. "He's got to build back that blood he lost." The Doc and Buck went out on the porch.

"Aren't you glad you're not young and foolish?" Doc Bell grinned at Buck.

"Well I'm sure not young," Buck said.

Doc nodded. "Being foolish is not necessarily a preroga-tive of the young," he agreed. "But you've always seemed to be a most judicious man, Sheriff. Guess I'll go back down-town. Too lonesome at my place for an old widower like me. I'll be back to see Bud in the morning if he don't need me before then."

Buck nodded laconically. Doc picked up the half round weight to which his horse had been tied, tossed it in the buggy floor, and climbed in. He "chuck-chucked" the chest-nut around and out of the yard while Buck mounted Chalky.

The sheriff sat for a moment, watching Doc Bell drive off. Buck was convinced that he had no choice other than to fol-low Mark Jellico's and the ministerial alliance's recom-mendation. He was going to have to hire a special oilfield deputy. No telling how long Bud might be laid up. But the sheriff considered the thought that he might be foolish in wiring Hynote. His old Wyoming sidekick was courageous, no doubt about that.

As Buck rode thoughtfully out of the yard, he was recall-ing the Flagg wagon on the KC ranch. He was certain Hynote had been one of those who had backed it, blazing with pitch pine and hay, into the KC ranch house to drive Champion out into the yard.

Hynote had also been one of the men who had manned the advance trench at the $\overline{\text{A}}$ ranch, ready to provide the hail of bullets that had pursued the go-devil after it had passed them. No one with sense could doubt Hynote's courage. He would make his presence known at Cimarron Bend in a hurry. But Buck found himself hoping Hynote had matured some since the Johnson County fracas. Another deputy as precipitous and hair-triggered as Bud Reed could be disastrous.

A few more people were on the street now that the circus was out. Mostly men, gathered in groups, talking, and Buck suspected the latest exploit of their sheriff and his deputy was the subject of most of these conversations. He waved at friends here and yonder as he rode directly through the town, and to the depot.

Dismounting and going inside, he told the Santa Fe station agent, "Give me a telegraph blank, Ed. I want to send a night letter."

III

Hynote was due to arrive on the 2:35 train from Wichita
the next afternoon. Bud wouldn't stay in bed and insisted
that he felt well enough for light duty, so Buck asked him to
meet the train. Buck gave his deputy detailed instructions
while Bud listened, his sun-darkened face alert and atten-
tive.

"You're looking," Buck said, "for a tall, slender gent—
handlebar mustache, unless he's shaved it off since last I saw
him. Steel blue eyes that will bore a hole in you, and a hard,
thin-lipped mouth. He won't smile much. But he'll talk.
Quite a bit if I remember him right, and mostly about himself. And damn it, Bud, whatever he says, don't argue with
him! Best I remember, he's never lost an argument, right *or*
wrong.

"His name is Hyman Knote," Buck said. "It's a kind of
awkward name, and we got to calling him Hynote. But don't
start off with that. You better call him Mr. Knote. Go by the
livery stable and rent one of Talmadge's hacks. Show him
the town. Buy him a cigar. Explain to him that we're in the
Indian Territory and under prohibition. Otherwise you'd
buy him a drink.

"Tell him I'd have been there myself to meet him, but
I've got to meet with that confounded Ministerial Alliance
and Judge Hull's Betterment League—they'll have me on the
griddle all afternoon. If I remember Hynote right he
wouldn't sit still for such palaver for thirty minutes let alone
three hours.

"Bring him by the house about six. Kaahti is cooking supper for us all—you're invited, of course. After supper I'll take him over to Cimarron Bend and see how he likes his prospective bailiwick."

The settlement of Cimarron Bend was on the north side of the river, fourteen miles, over section line roads, from Logan Station. The main road skirted a mile west of the hollow where Buck and Bud had captured Wiley Lester the previous Saturday night. That narrow track dead ended at the river, below the same bluffs where the Dalton gang had once hid out in a cave big enough to hold several tons of hay.

A half mile farther around the river's big bend was Horsethief Canyon, a blind canyon well hidden and accessible only from the river. There the Daltons had been accustomed to hold horse herds stolen in Texas, later to be herded on to Kansas, where the horses could be sold to farmers not too curious about the source of the livestock they bought from the outlaws at bargain prices.

The main road, over which Sheriff Mather and his new deputy, Hyman Knote, now lurched in Buck's T-Model was deep rutted, swirling with dust in the early evening dusk and lined with horse freight rigs.

"The oilfield commences at Cimarron Bend," Buck told Hynote, "and spreads on north for ten-twelve miles. There's never a time, day or night, when there's any less traffic on this road. The railroad is building across to Cimarron Bend, but it lacks eight miles of getting there yet. So all the freight, rig timbers, casing, boilers, drill pipe and the like has to come from the Santa Fe freight yard in Logan Station.

"There'll be five hundred teams of four to a dozen horses and mules loading up at the Santa Fe yards in Logan Station every morning. Mule skinners and teamsters cussing till

hell won't have it. All trying to set a new record for the trip
to the oilfield and back."

Hynote was clinging grimly to the door edge and the seat
back of the car as it jumped from rut to rut.

"More money changing hands here than in the Virginia
City goldrush," he guessed.

"Right," Buck affirmed. "This oilfield has already produced more money than Virginia City did, and it's hardly
started."

"A sure enough bonanza," Hynote marveled. "No wonder
you've got every card shark and highjacker west of the Mis-
sissippi gravitating in here."

The Ford threaded its way among bell-jangling teams
tugging their loaded wagons toward the river bridge ahead.

"What happens when it rains?" Hynote asked.

"Turns this road into a hub deep gumbo of red clay mud."
Buck raised his voice to a near shout to combat the jingling
and harness noise of the freight teams funneling in toward
the bridge. "More freighters get bogged down than move in
that kind of mud. We sure wouldn't be coming through here
in this hossless carriage after a rain."

Buck had felt a lift of reassurance when he had first seen
Hynote. He had been surprised at how much Hynote had
aged, and perhaps with age had come some wisdom. Hynote
was fifty. He had been five years older than Buck during the
Johnson County War's fighting, and ten times more reckless.
Surely a man with Hynote's experience-lined countenance
had lived out his reckless days and would now undoubtedly
be steady and reliable.

The conversation during supper had been carried mostly
by Bud, recounting what Hynote had told him during the
afternoon about Hynote's and Buck's adventures in Johnson
County, Wyoming. Buck had remembered it all somewhat
differently, but was inclined to take his own earlier advice
about not arguing with Hynote, who he knew well enough
could be dogmatic, arbitrary, and opinionated.

Hynote had during the afternoon told Bud the story of
the killing in Johnson County of Nick Ray and Nate Champion—how their posse of noble and right-minded ranchers
had run down the rustlers Ray and Champion in the KC
ranch house on Powder River. They had killed Ray during
the shootout during their siege of the log cabin ranch house
where Ray and Champion had holed up.

When Champion had refused to surrender they had made
a go-devil out of a nester's wagon, loaded it with hay and
pitch pine, set it afire and backed it up against the ranch
house.

The burning of the ranch house had smoked out Champion, who was killed trying to escape. That was hardly how
Buck recalled the sickening affair. Both he and Hynote had
been with the raiding force, which numbered close to sixty
men. The Wyoming settlers had called them "invaders."
Only about half the raiders were Wyoming ranchers. The
rest were hired gunfighters.

Both Buck and Hynote had been among the hired
members of the war party. They and their horses had been
hauled out from Denver to Casper on a fast special train
hired for that purpose. At Casper they had joined the Wyoming ranchers and set forth on a cold April night as an extra-
legal raiding force. That there had been some cattle rustling
in Johnson County there could be no doubt. But only part of
the trouble was rustling. The rest involved small settlers
trying to hang on to their little ranches in the face of over-
whelming pressure from Wyoming's land barons.

The charges that Nick Ray and Nate Champion were cattle thieves should have been left to the courts to judge. They
had been given no such chance. Ray had been killed inside
the KC cabin by the hail of lead shot into it by the besiegers
surrounding it on the outside. Champion had put up a he-
roic fight, only to be driven out when the raiders set the log
cabin afire.

Buck had never been able to forget the twisting and turning of Champion's body as uncounted bullets had hit him when he ran from the burning house. He had never been able to forget that some of the raiders kept shooting into Champion's body after he was dead and lying on the ground.

Buck still recalled short passages from the diary that had been found on Nate Champion's body after he was dead, Champion's short account, kept during the overnight siege; "Nick is shot, but not dead yet," it had said. "He is awful sick. I must go and wait on him." This was written by a lone man surrounded by near sixty men, all determined to kill him.

Over the years since Johnson County, Buck had tried to forget the words Nate Champion had written. "Boys, I feel pretty lonesome just now . . ." and later "I think they are going to fire the house . . . the house is all afire. Goodbye, boys, if I never see you again."

As a result of such remembrance, Buck had never been able to forget the grim Johnson County War. Champion's courageous words had become indelible in his memory no matter how hard he tried to forget them, and Buck had long ago made one hard resolution. Never again would he be a part of any vigilante or "enforcer" outfit that set forth outside the law, however justified they felt their motives to be.

Nor would he permit vigilante or "enforcer" activities to go on in any place where he had the legal responsibility of enforcing the law. And his doubts earlier this evening had in part sprung from wondering if Hynote would go along with any such high-minded ideas.

But as the evening had worn on, with supper over and the dishes cleared away, Buck had spent his coffee drinking time studying Hynote's thin, aging face. It was seamy with wrinkles that ought to indicate the sobering experience gained from years of hard living. Hynote had not talked a lot, Bud Reed's mouthiness had seen to that, but Hynote's comments from time to time had seemed tempered and reasonable.

Buck decided to shed his lingering doubts and give his old sidekick a chance. He had sworn Hynote in, and filled out and signed his commission papers as special oilfield deputy. They had cranked up the Ford and started for Cimarron Bend. Now they sat waiting in line for their turn to cross the Cimarron River Bridge.

The wooden bridge was a half mile long, a rambling and crooked structure that looked like it could hardly bear its own weight, let alone the steady procession of freight wagons bound for Cimarron Bend, and the empties that deadheaded back across it.

Buck finally managed to thread the Ford into the slow line of traffic and they crept out onto the bridge's rattling floor boards. Bridge timbers trembled beneath them as they eased across the shallow, salty stream below them. Shrouded by the night as it was, its slow current glistening in the light of an almost full moon, sided by dark sandbars that tapered off to infinity, the Cimarron looked ominous.

But Buck knew it was probably no more than a foot deep anywhere across its meandering width. There was quicksand down there, and if the bridge gave way under them, they would surely lose the car. But their own fate could hardly be anything worse than having to wade ashore in the murky knee deep water.

The T-Model kept chugging along, Buck's left foot depressing the low gear pedal, and presently they were across. Here the road widened. He ginned her up to a higher speed, passed the wagon before them, and let out the pedal to shift to high gear. Once more they were kicking up dust, jouncing across the ruts, passing the slow moving freight outfits, and the silhouettes of Cimarron Bend's ramshackle frame buildings loomed before them against the flicker of gas waste flares in the oilfield beyond the town.

It was a false-front town of a single street, its residence area wandering off along paths and byways as yet unorganized into any pattern or system. Along the single street were

the oilfield supply houses, rig-timber yards, blacksmith
shops, stores, and amusement joints necessary to outfit the
oilfield, and keep its workers entertained.

One of these was the Folly Theatre, and as Buck turned
right at the corner in front of it he noted that the Folly's
foyer was thoroughly pasted up with show bills, all proclaim-
ing—in two words only—tonight's show attraction. The two
words on every poster, in red letters about a foot high, were
RUBY PICKARD. Buck found a place to crowd the Ford in
beside the board sidewalk a long two hundred yards around
the corner from the Folly's entrance.

Buck and Hynote got out and as they walked back toward
the main street they could hear the whoopla erupting vol-
canically from the thin wooden walls of the barnlike show-
place.

Hynote commented, "Sounds like tonight's show must be
a rouser."

"Always is when Ruby Pickard's on stage," Buck said.
"She'll hit town in a breezy, firehouse style and make a couple passes through main street in that bright red Oakland
she drives. Then she parks in front of some pool hall, goes
in, and does the shimmy on top of a pool table. In the win-
tertime she wears a big fur coat, and sees to it that the word
gets around town that 'Ruby ain't wearin' nothin' under that
fur coat.'"

They turned the corner and Hynote stopped before the
theater foyer. It was late enough for the show to be almost
over. The ticket booth stood empty. In it, propped up behind the ticket wicket, was a sizable show card reading
"Don't miss Ruby's stupendous return performance—Thurs-
day night of this week—all new songs, new dances, new
acts."

"Ruby's a real performer, and a good girl," Buck opined.
"Last Christmas she had a show scheduled here and some
skunk stole all the Christmas presents she'd bought for her
show troupe. Ruby came over to Logan Station, borrowed

money from the Gray Brothers' Bank and replaced every
present."

"An oilfield sweetheart," said Hynote.

Buck nodded.

Hynote said, "Let's go in."

They entered the theater. The finale was in progress and
Ruby was on stage, coyly decked out in a modish dress
circled with wide vermilion stripes. Full at the hips, the
dress decreased in circumference to become a hobble about
her pretty ankles. She was twirling a parasol to match the
dress, and her chorus line of six shapely girls was high-kick-
ing to the sultry song Ruby warbled coquettishly, with
saucy, flippant gestures of body and hips.

Hynote whispered hoarsely, "I expect about everybody in
town is in here."

"The whole sporting crowd, anyway," Buck agreed. "The
gamblers, the card sharks, the bootleggers—"

But Hynote was already out of hearing distance, striding
down the aisle toward the stage. The new oilfield deputy
reached the end of the aisle and climbed up the steps to the
stage. Hynote struck a belligerent pose, standing, stage-
center, facing the audience directly in front of Ruby Pickard's dancing and singing. He pulled his .45 from the holster
and fired twice into the scenery flies overhead.

The gunfire brought the act, the music, the noisy audience to a halt and a thick silence fell throughout the theater.
Hynote spoke. His voice was rough with threat, loud, and
carried harshly into every corner of the packed theater.

"My name is Hy Knote," he told the audience. "Sheriff
Buck Mather has just appointed me special deputy to take
care of this town and the oilfield north of here." Hynote slid
his long smokepole six-shooter back in its holster. "Now I
heard that this town is the roughest place in the county. But
that's over and done with. I came here to clean it up—and I
brought a mighty dangerous fellow to help me," he made a

lightning fast draw of the .45 hogleg on his hip and fired another shot into the painted scenery above him.

As Hynote vaulted down off the stage the audience sat in stunned silence for a long minute, then, as the talk began to swell, the musicians in front of the stage made a lame effort to pick up the song Ruby had been singing where she had left off.

The music limped along badly for a few bars. Buck followed Hynote back into the Folly's foyer, and by the time they were again on the wooden sidewalk outside the theater, the orchestra had begun to find its beat. Ruby Pickard had started to sing again, but her song sounded more scared than sexy.

"Let's go back and get my suitcase out of your car," Hynote suggested. "You can go on back to Logan Station. I'll take over from here."

He seemed not only confident. He seemed cocksure.

Buck hesitated. "Let's find you a rooming house first, Hynote," he suggested. "I ought to introduce you to Barney Arles and a few other men around town here."

"I've done introduced myself," Hynote said thinly. "No use of you wasting time hanging around here. I'll make out in good shape. You go on back to your big town."

Though a good deal more than doubtful now, Buck started.

Convinced that he ought at least to advise somebody of Hynote's presence in town, on the way back to his car Buck paused at The Same Old Ikey's Saloon. It was running wide open as usual as Buck walked in and elbowed his way up to the long, crowded bar.

Summoning the attention of a fat, dirty aproned bartender, Buck demanded, "Where's Price?"

"He ain't here," shrugged the bartender swabbing the bartop in the immediate area in front of Buck. "He usually goes out to eat around this time."

Buck walked on back to his Ford, and drove out to Arles'

Casino on the edge of town. Entering the busy gambling house, Buck stood eying the dice tables, listening to the roulette croupier's chant and the clacking spin of Arles' big wheel of fortune. Spotting the floor manager then, Buck went to him to ask, "Barney in his office?"

"No, sir," the Casino floor manager said politely. "Ikey Price came by for him in his new Maxwell, maybe an hour ago. I figure they probably drove over to Logan Station to eat supper."

Buck stood for a moment, then gave up altogether. As he drove back to Logan Station he realized that, in spite of his caution, he might have been too hasty in swearing Hynote in. But it was too late now. Nothing to do but give Hynote a chance, and keep a careful eye on the situation. *There is the possibility,* Buck thought, *which I've got to face up to, that Hynote may be harder to ride herd on than the town he is supposed to regulate.*

When Buck arrived back in Logan Station, he drove directly to the courthouse. It was past 2:00 A.M., and it seemed like a long time since he had crawled out of bed just before noon. *Long hours and low pay,* he thought, as he turned the knob and went in through the back door of his office. The place was quiet, as it should be. Shorty Long would have gone off duty quite a while ago, and Lige Foley, the night jailer, should now be in charge.

Bud Reed would be sound asleep in the spare bedroom at Buck's own house, and Sheriff Buck Mather found himself feeling a little lonesome. Time to make a last check of the prisoners, then go home and turn in himself.

He opened the door that led into the jail corridor between the cells, and could hear snoring. There was only one prisoner besides Wiley Lester. A steady jail customer named Spunker who had been in and out of the territorial prison twice since Buck had become sheriff. This time he was being held on charges by the Anti-Horse Thief Association that he had stolen a spavined mule belonging to an aged Negro who made his living plowing and cultivating gardens in the spring, tending yards in summer, doing odd jobs in autumn, and hauling firewood for Logan Station residents in the winter.

Spunker was a heavy sleeper, and Buck was not surprised to hear him snoring, but he was surprised to see that Lige Foley was not at the jailkeeper's desk at the far end of the corridor between the cells. Buck walked on back into the jail.

At first he thought Wiley Lester's cell was empty, but it was not. Jailer Foley, unconscious, had been shoved under the cell's bunk. A little blood was still leaking from the wound where Foley's hair had been parted by a blow from something very solid. The cell door was locked, and Wiley Lester was gone.

IV

Buck fetched cold water in a dipper from the jail water bucket, untied Foley's red neckerchief and used it to bathe the jailer's wrinkled face. The old timer sat up.

"Take it easy, Lige," Buck cautioned.

Foley cursed dizzily and stood up. He staggered, leaned to grab the cell's bars and looked out into the corridor.

"Gone, huh?"

Buck nodded.

"Damn if you hadn't ought to fire me, Buck!"

Lige Foley's self-castigation clearly afforded him little relief. He swayed against the bars, took the water dipper out of Buck's hand, drank deeply from it, then went on. "I had just relieved Shorty Long. Shorty left through the jail office. I started walking back toward my desk. Lester's arm snaked out and had me hauled up before I could even holler. Hit my head on the bars when he heaved me in. I was so groggy that I barely remember him throwing his elbow around my Adam's apple to shut off my wind. He took my gun and got my keys. I plumb don't remember him locking me in here and taking off, but it shore looks like he done it."

Buck thought about it. That would have been more than five hours ago. He went to the wall phone to telephone Sparky North at home, getting the sleepy mechanic out of bed. When North's drowsy answer finally stopped the telephone's ringing, Buck asked, "Sparky, did you bring in that car that was stalled out by Jake Vandergriff's place?"

"Un-huh," answered the sleepy mechanic.

"Good. Where is it?"

"Well, I took it to my shop downtown, but it ain't there now."

"You mean Lester's got it again?"

"Hell, no." The sleepy Sparky sounded testy. "It was a stolen car. Belonged to a driller named Cater, over at Cimarron Bend. I'd worked on it for him just last week. I called Cater, told him I had his car, and he came over this afternoon and got it."

Buck hung up disgustedly.

It took another hour for him to rouse Shorty Long out of bed, get him back down to the jail, and to find Doc Bell. Bell's jocular gratitude expressed to Buck for all the business the sheriff's force was providing him failed to amuse Buck. He left Bell shaving Lige Foley's pate bald around the bruised wound where Wiley Lester had parted the old man's thin hair with the jailer's own gun.

Buck took a futile turn through a few of Logan Station's darkened streets, not because he expected to find Wiley Lester, but just because it was the thing to do. He prowled the main part of town, holding a vague hope that Lester might have gotten hung up somehow, somewhere, in some strange set of circumstances that would produce either the outlaw or visible evidence of whatever trail he had taken.

But there was no way of knowing which way Lester might have gone, and entirely unlikely that he was anywhere within miles of Logan Station by now, so, shortly, Buck drove the Ford on down to the depot. Here he wired "wanted" information to law enforcement agencies in adjoining counties, and to the Peace Officers' Association at the territorial capital.

Exhausted, Buck went home, hoping to catch a few hours' sleep in spite of his frustrations and smoldering concern. It was close to 5:00 A.M. when he stepped silently into the bedroom, moving as noiselessly as he could. But on his quiet entry Kaahti, suddenly and abruptly, sat bolt upright in bed.

"Kaahti," Buck said in low-spirited depression and dismay, "I'll swear I was being even quieter than usual."

"It was no sound you made that brought me awake," she said. Reaching across her bedside table, she struck a match, lifted the lamp chimney, and lit the wick.

Buck looked at her closely, long aware of her uncanny skill at sensing when he was going through troubled times. He stepped to open the wardrobe cabinet, extracted his nightshirt, and began the routine chores of getting into it, telling her:

"That prisoner we had—Wiley Lester—the one that held up the Odeon cashier—escaped tonight."

She was entirely awake now, watchful, scrutinizing him searchingly, waiting. Buck paused in the act of pulling out his shirttail.

"How's Bud?" he asked.

Kaahtidoah swung her pretty feet free of the bed and reached to slip them into the petite beaded moccasins she still preferred to wear instead of houseshoes. Buck had observed how well she had adapted to the mores and manners of the white woman's world in all her daily and social contacts with it, and the comfortable ease with which she slipped once more into the familiar Indian ways of her youth inside the closed doors of privacy in her own home.

Now, instead of a bathrobe, she reached to the foot of the bed for a light Pendleton blanket of sky blue and white stripes which she draped with gentle grace about her shoulders. "Bud is gone," she said. "There is no use trying to persuade that young warrior to behave himself and rest. It would be easier to persuade a wild buffalo calf to lie down, and it will never do that even if it is wounded."

"When did he leave?" Buck asked.

"Right after noon," she said. "I was able to feed him beef and cheese for lunch. But he said he refused to be a burden on me. He drove me from the room by threatening to dress in front of me if I didn't leave. He shut me out, put on his clothes, and left."

"Where did he go?" Buck pulled the nightshirt down over his head and worked at unbuckling his belt beneath it.

"To that room at the Saddle Rock Hotel, where he lives, I expect," she said. "He will lie there, hidden, a little while, then rise to fight again. But he will never lie down where anyone can see him, or lie down and stay, unless he is so wounded that he cannot move."

Buck tugged off his boots and sat on the edge of the bed in his nightshirt, his hairy legs protruding beneath it, his bare feet taut on the bedroom's Persian rug. Looking down at his bare feet, he said, "Kaahti—"

She turned on the bed to look at him, directly, as aware of the depth of his concern as he.

Buck sat with slumped shoulders. "Do you remember the fourth day of April last spring?"

She frowned, studying. "In the evening?" she asked.

Buck nodded. "Along toward dark it got hot and sultry. Then big black clouds came a-boiling in from the southwest. They came this way slow, but a-rolling."

"Yes," she said, "and soon there was no air. I could hardly breathe. The wind came up suddenly, and very cold. It rushed into the airlessness, shrieking and tearing, sweeping away the fresh leaves and even the green branches from the trees."

"Then came the tornado," Buck said. "They have never fully rebuilt the part of town that it took. They probably never will."

Kaahtidoah's eyes, distance focused, were remembering.

Buck said, "It laid flat those houses down there in the elbow of Cottonwood Crick as if they'd been gone over by a steam roller."

"Then came the hail," Kaahti recollected. "Falling stones of ice so big they killed cattle in the fields."

Buck still sat slumped, staring at the floor, "And a good

many people, too, lost their lives in that storm." Still he sat
unmoving. "That's what's going to happen when the Logan
Station Ministerial Alliance, and Caleb Hull's Civic Better-
ment League, butt heads with that loose living crowd that
Hynote is trying to get a grip on over at Cimarron Bend."
He exhaled deeply and lay down on the bed.

Kaahti looked down at him, mirroring his concern. From
sheer exhaustion, he seemed already to have fallen asleep.
She glanced out the bedroom window. Dawn was already
cracking the eastern horizon. Kaahti arose to blow out the
lamp. Drawing the window curtain closed then, she moved
quietly out of the bedroom.

Buck was up before noon, but still tired. After breakfast,
he drove the Ford, with its evil smelling exhaust, to his
office, and found that a committee of two had arrived to
wait upon him. It consisted of the Reverend Mark Jellico
and Judge Caleb Hull.

The Reverend Mark, fussy, pious, and pudgy, was pacing
the office between the gun rack and the potbellied stove.
Each time he reached the black stove, he circled meticulously to avoid the coal scuttle on the floor beside it, with
the chance it implied that he might get a little coal dust on
his carefully polished shoes.

Hull, a towheaded bumpkin who would never outlive the
rustic appearance of his hillbilly upbringing, stood in pompous asininity with his backside to the coal stove, even
though at past one o'clock on this warm late June afternoon,
the stove had contained no fire for almost three months.

The Reverend Mark smiled with waspish cordiality.
"Good afternoon, Sheriff. It does seem that, even for a public servant, you start your day's work rather late."

Judge Hull nodded majestically. "There has not been one
day in my entire life that I have not arisen before the sun."

Buck did not bother to tell them that he had managed to
get to bed for a little while only after the sun had already

arisen this morning. He said, noncommittally, "Good morning, gentlemen."

Judge Hull's yellow hair, lying thinly on his round, domed head, shifted fitfully in the currents of air stirred when Shorty Long suddenly opened the door connecting the office with the jail. Shorty, too, was red-eyed and weary looking from lack of sleep.

"Oh," he said. "You're here, Buck. These gentlemen have been waiting for quite a while. Lige called a while ago to say he was up and would be here directly. If you're gonna be here would you mind keepin' an eye on Spunker back here till Lige shows up? I shore need to go home and turn in."

"Sure, Shorty," Buck said mildly. "Leave that door standing open. What can I do for you gentlemen?"

Hull's shoulders were meaty with heavy muscles made from wrestling the handles of a mule-drawn plow for a good many years before his first election as a justice of the peace. That had led to his election as county judge. He had never spent a day in law school in his life.

Throwing back his round head in a gesture he assumed to be leonine and lordly, he intoned, "We have come, Sheriff Mather, on a praiseworthy mission. We want to extend to you our congratulations on the man you have secured to fill the deputy's post in Cimarron Bend. At our suggestion, of course."

The Reverend Jellico interrupted his pacing a cleanly distance from the dirty coal scuttle. He had an exultant and righteous gleam in his eye. "We hear that Deputy Knote has already begun conducting raids on Cimarron Bend's dens of sin."

Buck thought, with some comfort easing his weariness, *Well, he sure didn't waste any time.* Intending to contribute as little to the discussion as possible, in the hope that it might hasten this pair's departure, Buck sat down at his desk and laced his fingers together.

The silence hung, so Buck said, with a hint of finality in his voice, "Well, I thank you gentlemen for coming by."

The two staunch partisans of the right stood shoulder to shoulder now, with their pompous soft bellies thrust out at Buck, peering down at him through beetling brows of approbation.

"Delighted to do it, Sheriff Mather," Jellico said. "Our only suggestion now, and I believe Judge Hull will concur with me in this, is that you improve your own office hours. A public servant should be in his office, ready to answer to the needs of the taxpayers, certainly no later than eight o'clock each morning."

Buck grunted, and got to his feet, his tired thoughts trying to formulate a frank way to tell this pair to go to hell and still be reasonably proper and polite about it. But they were turning away to depart and Buck held his tongue in the conviction that their absence was entirely preferable to anything he might think of to say to them, however cleverly he might couch in words the caustic anger seething up through him.

The Reverend Mark and the Honorable Caleb reached the street door and opened it to confront two of the very denizens from the Cimarron Bend dens of sin they had just been denouncing.

Barney Arles, of Arles' Casino, had just been reaching for the doorknob. Beside him stood little Isaac Price, proprietor of The Same Old Ikey's Saloon. Arles, a tall and handsome man far more distinguished in appearance than either of the protagonists of righteousness he confronted, paused in midreach.

Barney Arles had the lordly mien that Judge Caleb Hull pictured himself as having, and so sorely lacked. But there was a vacuous emptiness in the handsome Arles' eyes. Looking at him, Buck thought, was like seeing the handsome façade of an architecturally impressive, but empty, building.

His companion, Ikey Price, was a little jittering monkey of

a man, nervously hopping from foot to foot. In height not quite reaching Arles' shoulder, a wizened, oily faced, unctuous appearing little man, he was virtually dancing with eagerness to enter the sheriff's office.

Somehow, Buck always expected Ikey Price to smell bad. There was an aura of stench, of evil odor, which seemed to exude from the little man, even though the odor did not in reality exist, and Buck always found himself surprised in Price's presence to find that Ikey Price didn't actually stink.

Like a tableau fixed for an instant in time, evil and righteousness stood confronted, the forces of evil outside the sheriff's office and eager to enter, the forces of virtue inside the office momentarily halted in their purpose of departure, now locked in face to face, eyeball to eyeball, struggle.

The Reverend Mark Jellico's finely veined nose flew skyward in shock, as if the stench of excrement had suddenly been deposited beneath his nostrils. Nose high, with only his incensed eyebrows higher, Mark Jellico plunged between the pair and out onto the sidewalk. Judge Caleb Hull, solemnly stolid, thrust his way out behind Jellico as the stern of a ship follows its prow, splitting Arles and Ikey Price even more widely apart.

Price leaped nervously on into Buck's office without a backward glance toward the departing pair. Barney Arles, half a pace behind Ikey, came in. His distinguished mien anxious and disturbed, he literally cried out in anguish, "Buck, what in the hell have you done to us?"

"Yes, yes," jabbered the little saloonkeeper, "what in the hell!"

Buck, again seated at his desk, fingers interlaced, studied the distraught pair. "All right," he said agreeably, "what in the hell have I done to you?"

"It's that man! That deputy! Hynote!" Price sputtered and stuttered, his wrinkled simian hands gesturing wildly in the fine spray of his own spit.

"Right!" Barney Arles confirmed heavily.

Buck leaned back in his swivel chair. "I heard he's already raided you boys."

"Raided?" A look of horror crept across Arles' handsome face.

The broad shouldered, deep-chested, Adonis of professional gamblers stalked across the room to halt directly in front of Buck's chair, his horror mixed with wrath as he declared, "Your so-called deputy, this Hynote, came into my place about closing time last night. He told my casino banker, just as calm as you please, to count him out a hundred dollars in greenbacks. Next he come up to me and told me to have another hundred just like it ready for him when I got ready to open up every Monday night. Any Monday without that hundred dollars would be the beginning of a week in which my casino would be closed up tight."

Buck said nothing. He just sat, wanting to think about this. Which was just as well because Ikey Price was still hopping up and down like a small boy who has waited too long in responding to a call of nature.

"He hit me this morning! The very first thing!" sputtered Ikey. "Opened my cash register himself without so much as a by-your-leave! And along with the hundred dollars he relieved me of, he walked around behind my back bar, picked himself a case of my best imported Irish whiskey and hoisted it up on his shoulder."

A slow numbness began to fill Buck Mather. It was like some foreboding, deep in his subconscious, had taken sudden, visible shape.

"Well, boys," he said, postponing its recognition. "I guess I'll have to get over there, won't I?"

"Get over there?" exploded Ikey. "I want my money back! And my whiskey!"

Buck locked eyes with the monkey-like little saloonkeeper. "Price, you've got a gall that would sicken a stable hand," he charged. "I know that you boys worked hard for my election, and that without Cimarron Bend's votes I wouldn't even have this job. But there you sit, in the Indian Territory, where prohibition is the law of the land, operating a wide-open saloon as easy-come easy-go as if you were running it in New York's Bowery. You're breaking the law as offhanded as a liar breaks a promise, and you expect me to give you protection in it?"

Ikey Price immediately turned obsequious, unctuous. "Well, now Sheriff, you know how it is. In a boomtown like Cimarron Bend the whiskey is bound to flow ever easier than the oil. I'm not the only one over there selling it."

"You're the only one selling it over a mahogany bar with a brass rail to put your foot on, and a crystal chandelier hanging overhead to make a pretty reflection in your back-bar mirror," Buck told him. "And you, Barney"—Buck turned to the handsome casino owner—"you figure the law ought to provide protection for you and your gambling games? Everything you're doing is illegal."

Arles frowned servilely, becoming suavely ingratiating as he protested, "Oh, Buck, you know that oilfield hands are a wagering crowd. If I wasn't running some games they'd be finding plenty of things to bet their money on. At least I give them an honest shake for their money. And you're going to need our help in the next election as bad as you needed it in the last one."

Buck was leaning forward, nodding his head as he stared grimly at the floor, "Honest shake? Shakedown, maybe!"

"Now I don't like to hear you say that, Buck," Barney Arles objected. "You know that every game I run is honest. And you know you've turned a shakedown artist loose on us."

Ikey Price nodded jerkily.

Buck was still staring at the floor. "I expect I know it now," he admitted. "But I didn't know it before."

"And you can be damn sure he'll be shaking down Etta Redmond and her girls," Barney Arles declared smoothly.

"I expect so," Buck agreed. "I'm sorry, boys. I sent Hynote over there to regulate you, but not to rob you." Buck stood up suddenly. "What in the devil am I apologizing to you for? Get out of here! Both of you!"

V

After Barney Arles and Ikey Price had left his office, Buck again sat down, dejected. Some sixth sense had been warning him that Hynote and Cimarron Bend could make a volatile mix. He had expected the old rascal to do a few precipitous things, perhaps not always to show the best judgment in the world, but he had not anticipated anything like this.

Open graft and bribery. With rising anger he drove to Cimarron Bend to hunt up Hynote. He was not long in finding him. As Buck drove into town, on his first pass down the main street, he spotted Hynote leaning on a post which supported a crudely lettered sign at the corner of Cimarron Bend's principal intersection.

The sign advertised *Singers' Clothing Store: Everything in Men's Wear; Army Goods: Tents and Cots.* Hynote leaned, balding but dapper, holding his hat in his left hand, his right, as always, close to his low-slung .45, its holster tied down. Buck noted that passers-by tended to walk around him, giving him a wide berth. Hynote had clearly lost no time in cultivating a reputation.

Buck turned in to park, bouncing his Ford's left wheels across a half-buried gas pipeline that lay along the edge of the dirt street. He shut her down and got out. Hynote saw him immediately and lifted his hat in a friendly hail.

"Howdy, Sheriff. Fine day, ain't it?"

Buck approached, nodding in agreement. It was a fine day, cloudless, abundant sunshine, and a pleasant June afternoon breeze. Hynote took Buck's arm as he came up alongside.

"Come with me, Buck. I've got something I want to show you."

They walked around the corner. What Hynote wanted to show was parked beside a gasoline pump with a high glass globe that said *Filtered Gasoline*.

"I bought me a motorsickle," Hynote said proudly.

There it sat, shiny black, wire wheeled, with sidecar attached.

"Git in," Hynote invited.

"To go where?" Buck asked.

"To my place," Hynote replied. "I've got some more I want to show you."

Buck climbed in the sidecar, screwed his hat down tight, and they took off. It was a wild ride, but short. Up out of the paper littered roadside ditch, across ruts of hard dried mud, down to wheel around the far corner, scattering pedestrians and hastening the pace of an ambling cur dog, to lurch up and stop short in front of the Cimarron Bend Boarding House.

"I was lucky," Hynote said. "Ran into a fellow who said he was moving out of this boarding house right after you left town the other night. I hustled down here and rented his room. Come on in."

Lucky is right, Buck thought. In this crowded oilrush town a man was lucky to find a cot in a flophouse that he could rent for twelve-hour shifts. Men were sleeping at night on pool tables in the pool hall. Hynote had a boarding house room here complete with bed, washstand, and basin, even a scaly mirror hanging on the wall.

On the floor, beside the strewn clutter of Hynote's open suitcase, stood two standard slot machines.

"This is what I wanted to show you," Hynote declared. He toed the slot machine around with his boot, removed four loosely set corner screws, and removed the back. "Looky here. Set to pay off four to one in favor of the house. I raided that Arles' Casino late last night. I told Arles no more slots, and I intend to keep a close eye on every game he runs. Any crookedness and I'll shut him down tight."

An opened case of Irish whiskey was on the other side of Hynote's unmade bed. Buck nodded toward it. "You going to throw a party?"

Hynote laughed genially. "I confiscated it from that saloon The Same Old Ikey's. It's the same old poison. Taste that stuff, Buck! Imported Irish whiskey!" Hynote snarled derisively. "That stuff's laced with fusel oil."

Buck picked up the opened bottle by Hynote's bed and tasted it. It was bad whiskey all right, but Buck noted that Hynote had had to drink three fourths of the quart to be sure.

"I told Price," Hynote said, "not to label anything imported anymore unless he had invoices to show me to prove it. Buck, I don't want to shut this town down tight. Do that and this whole end of the county will vote against you next election. But I sure intend to keep these jaybirds honest."

Buck eyed Hynote directly, and his new deputy returned the stare without blinking. *All right*, thought Buck, *now I've got two stories, theirs and his. Maybe I need to look a little farther*.

"Mind if I walk around town awhile, Hynote?" Buck asked.

"Help yourself, Buck. Now that I'm here I think I'll lay down and nap awhile. It's apt to be a long night."

As Buck walked out on the front porch he encountered the boarding house's broom-wielding landlady. She let Buck walk past, and almost to the corner of the house before she caught up with, and stopped him.

"Sheriff," she hissed. "Am I supposed to put up with this?"

Buck halted. "Put up with what, missus?"

"That deputy of yours. He came here last night and ran off Abner Hilton, the roughneck that was renting that front room nights. Elmer Ryland, who has been sleeping in it days, he ran him off this morning. I'm getting one rent out of that room now instead of two—"

"Missus . . . ?" Buck removed his hat.

"Riley," she informed him.

"Missus Riley, are you renting every room in your place twice?"

"I sure am."

"Then I'm sure you won't starve while I check some things out."

Buck proceeded on down the street. His earlier anger now somewhat diluted by confusion, he pointed himself in the direction of Etta Redmond's Green Tree. Had Hynote really solicited graft from Arles and Price, or were they, in collusion, making that vicious charge because they were sore over Hynote's confiscation of the fixed slot machines and the bad whiskey?

They had sure convinced him during their diatribe in his office. Buck had thus far avoided directly accusing Hynote, simply because he figured he'd only get a direct denial, and be no farther ahead than he was. Maybe the truth was somewhere towards the middle.

Etta Redmond's house of ill fame The Green Tree, grew on the flat a quarter mile beyond the Folly Theatre. The "green tree" itself actually existed. It stood in front of the Queen Anne style ranch house now occupied by Etta and her girls. The old ranch house had once been headquarters for the sprawl of acres that had constituted the Turkey Track ranch before the oil discovery surrounded it with a forest of derricks to the north. The oilfield had spawned the clutter of oilfield supply houses and increased the litter of shack beaneries, stores, and joints that had long been called Cimarron Bend.

The oilfield had turned the Turkey Track's pastures black with oil waste, driving the cattle northwest into the Cherokee Strip where the grass still grew green. The "green tree" namesake of Etta's house, was a gnarled and ancient cedar, its original cone shape lost in a shaggy outgrowth of the boughs of old age.

Neither was it any longer green. It was gray-green, in part from age, and in part from the fact that eight or ten gushers had come in wild to the north of it during the past winter. The black spew of sulphurous crude oil they had belched forth from the earth's bowels had been caught in the high and bitter winds of blue northers, the arctic storms sweeping down across the Great Plains.

These icy winds caught the gushing oil, whipped it into a frothy spray, and swept the oily mist before them to stain everything in its path. The coating of grime and grease the cedar tree had accumulated was slowly killing that ancient veteran of many Indian Territory winters.

The oil spray had had its effect on the big Turkey Track ranch house too, changing it from the sparkling white it had been when longhorn cattle had grazed within seeing range of its gabled, dormer windows. Now it was a speckled, muckledy-duck hue, infinitely more drab than any of the hookers who occupied it.

The Green Tree's girls were a colorful lot. Their boss lady, Etta Redmond, was even more colorful, attractive, and vivacious than any of the girls she employed. She was climbing into her surrey as Buck approached the house.

Her surrey was one to behold. Standing before the sweeping curve of the former ranch house's generous veranda, the surrey's shiny top, encircled with red ball fringes, sparkled in the afternoon sunlight. The surrey's fringes jiggled in the wind. Its red enameled exterior was neatly highlighted with fine yellow stripe-lines. Its spoked wheels were backing and filling with the nervous impatience of Etta's team of black, shiny-groomed carriage horses. Their tails were braided, as were the manes decorating their graceful necks, kept highly arched by curb bits. Topaz rhinestones decorated the bridles and harness with which Etta's porter was trying to control them.

Logan Station's strait-laced ladies had been scandalized when Etta's surrey had turned up as a part of that staid community's last Fourth of July parade. The two-seated surrey, adorned with its quivering fringe and bright paint, had been laden with a bevy of Etta's girls, all decked out in their lavish finest, twirling colorful parasols and flirting shamelessly with Logan Station men along the crowded curbside, who, one might say, "knew them well."

Etta spied Buck coming just as her porter urged the team into motion. She reached to tap the black man on the shoulder with her fan, stopping the carriage. Etta got down promptly and came walking to meet Buck. She was a statuesque woman with a gorgeous head of red hair, atop which was pinned a modish hat purchased in some place far more exotic than Cimarron Bend, or even Logan Station.

As they came together, she about-faced prettily, locked arms with him, and said, "Well, welcome, Sheriff. Surprise, surprise!" With a wave of her hand she dismissed porter and carriage. "Come in," she urged. "I don't believe you've ever seen the inside of my place."

She guided him up a recently built outside stairway to what was clearly her private entrance. Beyond its small entry hall, through a hanging curtain of golden topaz beads, which Buck noted exactly matched the decorative rhinestones on her carriage harness, lay a richly furnished parlor.

Passing through the beaded curtain, and holding it open for Buck, she invited, "Sit down."

Buck allowed himself to sink into the comfortable softness of an overstuffed chair, dropped his white Stetson beside it, and watched Etta, with hip-swinging motion of tasteful grace, walk across the expensive brocaded carpet and open an ornate liquor cabinet. The portrait of a reclining nude hung on the wall above the liquor cabinet. Though it caught his attention sharply, at first glance it seemed like every

other nude portrait he had ever seen hanging over a saloon
bar.

He recalled the women in those other portraits—pink-
fleshed and buxom, with full curved hips and rosy tipped
breasts—and then Buck's face began to turn pink and warm
as he realized that this nude portrait was a portrait of Etta
Redmond herself.

There was no mistaking the picture's facial features, or
the red hair. It was Etta. The live Etta, standing below it,
leaned temptingly to reach into the liquor cabinet and
brought forth a bottle of whiskey. She poured him a hefty
drink without asking him whether he wanted one or not.

The scent of it drifted across the room to him, a fragrance
of good sour mash Bourbon. Etta poured herself an equal
portion, and handed Buck his glass. He tasted it and resisted
a powerful urge to smack his lips. It was as tasty as its scent
had been. Etta took a long pull from her own glass with a
softly groaning sound of appreciation.

Buck could hardly look at her without also looking at the
nude portrait, and he felt himself growing hot and sweaty.
He was relieved as she began to move about the room, but
her movements were slow and swaying, her skirt clinging to
the contour of her hips, her motion accentuating them and
virtually demanding comparison of the clothed contours
with the unclothed picture above the liquor cabinet.

She opened a humidor, extracted a fine Havana cigar, bit
off the end with her own white teeth, and brought the cigar
to insert it herself between Buck's lips. As she did so she
brushed against him intermittently and the softness of her
sent Buck's eyes scurrying again to the portrait, then scurrying even faster away from it.

She lifted a silver cigar lighter from the knickknack table
beside him, thumbed its flint wheel, and leaned to apply the
flame to Buck's cigar. Her leaning gave him a deep and clear
view of her décolletage. Her bodice responded to the pull of
gravity and as Buck pulled on the cigar his eyes squirmed to

find some point of focus other than the deep cleft valley between the breasts before him, but it was hard.

Her fragrant sweet perfume swept over him, an intoxication more head-spinning than the fine Bourbon whiskey he was sipping and Buck fought for restraint and equilibrium. The moment was over then as Etta stood erect and began slowly moving about the room again, sipping her whiskey.

Sipping her whiskey, and flirting with him with her eyes, giving him a view of her figure from all angles, and the southern exposure was especially magnificent and memorable. Buck's blood was pulsing vigorously, he could feel it pulsing in his temples as Etta stopped, set down her drink, and removed the hatpin from her hat.

"I've met your new deputy, Buck," she said. "Personally."

She did not stop with the hatpin. She placed it on the table beside the chic hat it had formerly secured atop her flaming red coiffure, and casually began unbuttoning the cloth loops hooked over the buttons of her cashmere jacket. She slipped the jacket off and tossed it across the commodious back of a nearby couch.

"Someone must have pointed me out to him," Etta went on, "for he stopped me right after the Ruby Pickard show last night. He told me that my personal contribution to his weekly kitty would be one hundred dollars."

She was now, slowly, with graceful and tantalizing motion, removing her white and flouncy blouse. The blouse off, it joined the garment on the couch. Etta picked up her glass for another pull, winked at Buck, and said, "Great booze, isn't it?

"Since your Deputy Hynote hit me up," she added, "he's got around to most of the girls in the house, I think. At least three of them have told me they've been propositioned by him. I was just getting in my carriage for a drive to Logan Station to see you. I certainly appreciate your coming over."

Etta reached up to patiently remove a few hairpins. She

shook out her hair and it fell tumbling, a crimson cascade falling loose and lovely around her shoulders, white and bare now beneath the narrow chemise straps she had revealed in the striptease removal of her blouse.

Buck slid to the edge of the overstuffed chair, gripping his whiskey glass tensely.

"He hasn't propositioned any of my girls in the way you might expect," Etta commented. "I've got no reading on how horny the old goat is. He just told the girls to come across with ten dollars a week apiece or he'd see that they stayed off the street and entertained no guests."

She had unbuttoned her skirt and was slipping out of it now as Buck finally faced up to the reality that he was going to have to do something. A few more minutes, he fully realized, and she would be as naked as she lay there completely revealed in her portrait over the liquor cabinet.

He got hesitantly to his feet, saying, "Now, hold on there."

Buck's hands were shaking. As whiskey spilled, slopping over the edge of his glass, running down over his fingers and dripping onto the fine carpet, he said more firmly, "Hold it right there, ma'am. I got nothing on my mind but asking some questions, which it seems like you've already answered."

He forced himself calm, and put his half full whiskey glass down beside the one Etta had set on the table.

She stood, holding the half removed skirt, and smiled teasingly. "You *could* get your mind on something else, couldn't you?"

"Huh uh!" Buck declared. "I'm a married man."

Etta shaped her lips into a pretty little pout. "Sheriff, I'm a lot disappointed. Surely you don't really want to cut off the action just when the most exciting things are about to be revealed—"

"That picture," Buck interrupted, pointing at the nude portrait over the liquor cabinet, "is altogether revealing, and

while I wouldn't want to hurt your feelings, my wife Kaahtidoah has got you beat every way from the ace. Her face is
prettier, and so is the rest of her, and for just plain femi-
ninely womanliness—"

She cut him off by coming to lean against him. Buck
sucked in his breath.

"All right, true love," she said.

Her admiration for his loyalty to the Indian girl he had
married seemed to outweigh the pique she might have felt
at his rejection of her. "But," she frowned up at him, "you
will whistle up that mad dog you've sicked on us, won't you?
If you don't, a lot of us are going to think you're getting your
share of the graft he's collecting here."

Buck backed away, to retrieve his hat from the floor
where he had placed it. He put on the hat, backed through
the beaded curtain through which he had entered, and
crossed the small foyer to let himself out on the stair landing.

Downstairs, hurrying away from the house, walking back
along the rutted dirt road toward main street, Buck knew
that he was sweating all over. He pulled out his bandanna,
removed his hat, mopped away the perspiration beading his
brow, and said:

"Whew!"

VI

Buck walked thoughtfully on toward Cimarron Bend's main street. *What have I got*, he contemplated, and came up with the judicious answer: *I've got the testimony of a tinhorn gambler, a bootlegger, and a whore. All of whom could readily be conspiring to force me to get rid of Hynote. They're afraid he is going to force them out of business.*

Passing a blacksmith shop, Buck glanced into its smoky interior. A clock on the wall above the forge, with an advertisement for Brown's Mule Chewing Tobacco painted across its face, told him that it was close to five o'clock—getting late in the afternoon. Buck felt hungry. He took a look up and down the street and decided that Hynote must still be in his boarding house room, napping. At least he was nowhere in sight.

The sheriff turned toward a one-arm beanery with the appetizing name The Greasy Spoon, went in, sat at the counter, and ordered a bowl of chili. He consumed half a box of crackers and two glasses of milk with it to make sure it wouldn't rust out his stomach.

Stepping back on the street, he still saw nothing of Hynote. So he walked down to the Ford and climbed in, deciding to take a short turn out through the oilfield while he thought this over.

Half a mile north of town, where the forest of derricks really thickened, he saw the unstained rig timbers of a brand-new derrick, conspicuously in the process of spudding in.

The boom of the big spudding bit overrode all the oilfield
noise like the recurrent echo of a cannon fired over water.

Buck turned off the road and drove across the cattle
guard that defined the boundary line of the lease. Pulling
slowly up the anticline with the Ford in low gear, he eased
to a halt thirty or forty yards from the derrick to watch, and
think. The roaring gas burners under the boilers off to his
right sucked air as if they were trying to create a vacuum.
The oilfield air was permeated with the heavy stench of
crude oil and sulphurous gas.

To his left, beside the slush pit, the casing rack was
loaded with new six-inch pipe. The booming of the spudding bit reverberated above the hoarse labor of the engine
in its house of corrugated iron, half hidden in a cloud of exhaust steam. Every fall of the bit shook the whole derrick.

The fascination of what he watched temporarily drove
Hynote out of Buck's mind. It was a violent drama of man
against nature. In the midst of it, the driller leaned casually
against the headache post beneath the presently useless and
high-cocked walking beam, making hand signals to the tool-
dresser when he wanted the brake eased so the bullwheel
could add a few more inches of cable to the drilling string.

The derrick strained, its timbers creaking with every re-
morseless stroke of the pounding bit. The rig shook, its
crown block, sand line, bailer, floor, even the earth itself
shook. Buck estimated the huge bit must weigh half a ton,
attached to a ton and a half more of drilling stem, with another ton of steel jars above that.

As the band wheel turned, the jerk line hoisted the heavy
tools to drop them in successive rhythmic blows, pounding
their way down into the earth. Buck wondered how many
an oilfield murder went wholly undiscovered by the dropping of the body into that hole to be literally pounded into
disintegration by the raise and fall of the drill bit.

The driller had been hosing water down into the hole at
regular intervals, and now the drilling operation was

stopped while the bailer was run, sucking up the rock cuttings in the bottom of the hole and running them off into the slush pit. From the length of time it took to run the bailer to the bottom of the hole, Buck estimated the spudding bit had dug some thirty or forty feet of hole.

With a great whispering sound, the draw works ran again, heaving out the bailer, and the roustabout secured it in a corner of the derrick while the driller ran the tools back into the hole and set the spudding bit to work again. With long rehearsed routine, the three men on the drill floor, driller, tool-dresser, and roustabout, went about their chores, making haste in a measured and unhurried clockwork precision of movement that made something nearly ceremonious of this oil-stained, dirty, prosaic pageant, robbing of the earth its fossil fuel.

Buck's lost consciousness of time prodded him with the realization that almost an hour had passed, with him no closer to a decision as to what he ought to do than he had been when he had pulled up here. He heard a vehicle clatter across the cattle guard down the hill behind him. Turning around, Buck looked down the anticline to note that it was a work battered Ford roadster, with the back end cut out to convert it into a small jerry-built truck.

The strange looking little truck doodle-bugged up the hill to grind to a halt beside Buck, and its driver got out. The sheriff wondered if he was about to be ordered off the premises. He knew well enough that he was parked in a dangerous place. The violent strain on the draw works during a spudding operation is drastic, sometimes exploding a boiler from excessive steam pressure.

A snapped drilling string, any breakdown on a rig spudding in, is capable of shattering the derrick and turning the whole into a disaster of lashing cables, crashing timbers, and flying metal pieces.

The truck's driver, coming toward Buck, was a short, stocky-built, muscularly active man wearing khaki shirt, pants and high, laced boots. His clothes were too clean to be a working roustabout or roughneck, tool-dresser or driller. He wore glasses and had a look of authority about him. Buck decided he must be some kind of strawboss, a field supervisor.

Alongside Buck's door now, the short man asked, "You Sheriff Mather?"

Buck nodded.

"The fellow in the beanery in town said he thought he saw you head out this way. My name is Shaw. I'm the tool-pusher on this lease."

"Glad to meet you, Mr. Shaw," said Buck. "What can I do for you?"

"Well, by god, you can get two of my men loose so they can go to work tonight," Shaw said truculently.

"Loose from what?" Buck asked mildly.

"Loose from that son-of-a-bitch you've appointed deputy sheriff in Cimarron Bend." Shaw thrust his face, increasingly choleric as he talked, inside the car to confront Buck aggressively. "The off-tower toolie and driller working this rig went into town when they got off work at noon. They were tired as hell, like anybody is who has just put in a twelve hours' tower. They went into The Same Old Ikey's to have a few belts before they turned in. When they came out this scissorbill you've appointed deputy arrested them for public drunkenness. He says he won't turn them loose until each of them has paid him a fifty-dollar fine."

Arresting officer, judge, and jury, Buck thought at first, and then decided, *No, this is another case of straight-out bribery.*

Buck asked curiously, "Where's he holding them?"

Cimarron Bend had no jail.

"He's got them locked up in the doghouse at my own pipe yard," Shaw said. "He took my keys away from me at gunpoint. Said he'd give 'em back to me after the pair he's imprisoned have paid up."

That, in Buck's mind, settled it.

He thought this over briefly, feeling himself turn sour with depression as he again told himself he should have used more caution in checking Hynote out, less haste in appointing him. If Hyman Knote was going to prey on common oilfield workers, there was no longer any doubt. He had to go.

With a strong sense of self-reproach, Buck told the lease boss, "I'm sorry to hear about this, Mr. Shaw. Give me a little time and, the lord willing, I'll get this straightened out."

"How much time?" Shaw demanded.

"I'm heading into town right now," Buck said. "I'll try to have your men out in time for them to go back to work on their midnight tower."

Regretfully, Buck set throttle and spark, then got out and cranked the Ford. He backed up, and drove down the lease road. As he approached Cimarron Bend he gradually made up his mind. There was only one thing to do. Go back to Logan Station, find Bud Reed, and see if Bud felt up to making the drive back to Cimarron Bend with him.

If Buck stopped in Cimarron Bend now to charge Hynote and ask for his commission, he was certain to get one of two reactions. If Hynote was as guilty as it looked, there was sure to be a shootout. If, however, as impossible as it looked now, Hynote was innocent of the alleged briberies and graft, guilty of nothing worse than bad judgment, he would put up an argument in his own defense and try to justify his courses of action.

A guilty Hynote would be totally unwilling to resign. If guilty as charged by Barney Arles, Ikey Price, Etta Redmond, and tool-pusher Shaw, the old rascal Hynote would fight like a cornered coyote to hang on to the lucrative enterprise he had established here. The only way to prevent a killing would be to come at him with two men, separated far enough apart so that Hynote knew he could not possibly gun both of them down.

As Buck drove through Cimarron Bend's main street he spotted Hynote, leaning against the same post in front of Singers' clothing store where Buck had encountered him earlier in the afternoon. Hynote saw Buck's Ford coming, moved away from the post into the street, and waved at Buck as if expecting him to stop for palaver. Buck just waved back and kept on driving. He hoped that Hynote would accept it as a gesture of confidence. Maybe Hynote would think that Buck, seeing his Cimarron Bend deputy out and about and obviously ready for a night's work, would be reassured. He hoped that Hynote would be led to believe that Buck had just gone on his way, having full faith in him.

As the Ford slowly ate up the miles between Cimarron Bend and Logan Station, Buck let his thoughts drift and wander. He wondered what sort of shape he would find Bud in. The boy had gotten a pretty good clawing in the lions' cage, but youth usually heals quickly. Buck recalled the days only a couple years past when he had first become fully conscious of Bud Reed as a person.

It was right after Buck had first become sheriff. Bud was twenty years old then and seemed to be always hanging around the sheriff's office. He would help Shorty Long sweep out, carry meals to prisoners, anything to make himself handy, and Buck finally asked Shorty about him.

"The kid wants to be a lawman, Buck," Shorty had told him. "I've known him ever since he was a yonker. It's a kind of bad story. His own daddy wouldn't hardly have anything to do with him. From the time Bud was a tyke he was too much like his mother, too intelligent and too independent, for his old man to accept him. Floyd Reed was a handsome dude, but he never had brains enough for anything but common labor. He went to roughnecking in the oilfield as soon as it boomed. Bud's mother died when Bud was eighteen.

"Floyd Reed considered himself quite a gent. Seems like he judged his own manhood by the number of loose ladies he could sleep with, and it finally broke Bud's mother's heart. After she died, Floyd just got worse. I think it finally got through to him that it was his own orneriness that killed her. He got to staying drunk and finally went on tower that way one night. They were running casing and it was Floyd's job to work as derrick man, on the platform high up in the rig.

"He'd just had too much booze, got his feet tangled up wrestling a thribble and fell. He was dead as soon as he hit the derrick floor. Since then, Bud has worked at a lot of odd jobs. The boy worked at the Floradora Pool Hall for a while. Which used to make me worry about him because he was attracted to the reckless gambling gentry that hangs out there.

"I figured he'd get in trouble out of no more than his own reckless yen for adventure, so I started asking him to come over here to the jail and visit with me when I was on duty. Told him I was lonesome. He was always glad to help out with the sweeping up or whatever, but he needs a strong hand to guide him a-right."

The twenty-year-old Bud had reminded Buck a good deal of himself—of how he had felt and acted in those long past days when he had been twenty. So as soon as Bud had turned twenty-one, Buck had hired him and sworn him in as a deputy. There had been a few ticklish times since, for Bud's temper had a short fuse and his youthful judgment often lacked perspective.

But Buck had never really been sorry. Young Bud Reed was courageous, coming along fine, and Buck really felt full confidence in his young protégé. As the Ford crossed the rickety Cimarron bridge and continued jouncing from rut to rut, dodging through the steady procession of going and coming oilfield freight teams and trucks, Buck thought of his own days of hanging around the U.S. Marshal's office for the Western District of Arkansas, in Fort Smith.

He, too, had been a green kid eager to learn the ways of the lawman's trade. There were some important differences.

His dad had never rejected him; his old man had just felt
that Kentucky was getting too crowded and had moved his
family on west into Arkansas. The move itself had killed
Buck's dad. He had just been too far advanced in years for
another new frontier experience.

Buck had been left, at age seventeen, with three younger
brothers and sisters and a mother to support. He had done
it, working in a shoeshine parlor at night while wrestling
freight along the Arkansas River waterfront and in the
Frisco railroad freight yards during the daytime. It was
Heck Thomas who had taken an interest in him and per-
suaded old Hanging Judge Parker to put him on as a
deputy.

When Parker's court was split, with half its jurisdiction
going to Paris, Texas, Buck had gone with the Paris contingent. When the big money of the "enforcer" trip to fight for
the cattle barons in Wyoming's Johnson County War had
been offered, Buck had been unable to resist the temptation,
and went along. It took almost two years for the cattlemen
and their hired gunmen to get sufficiently free from the legal
entanglements resulting from the Wyoming fracas.

Buck had then returned to Paris, Texas, but there had
been nothing open for him there. He had drifted north into
the Indian Territory to Logan Station, where he got on that
frontier community's police force. Less than three years
later, he was the Chief of Police. A job he had held long
enough that, even now that he had been elected county
sheriff, half the local police force still came nearer to considering him still their boss than they did the new police
chief.

Buck often felt that he was, in a way, paying off his debt
to Heck Thomas by passing along that great officer's advice
and counsel to Bud Reed—"Never pull your weapon unless
you're ready and willing to use it. Never shoot at a man unless you're willing to kill him." Buck especially recalled the
time Heck had said, "I've never felt any pride in being

brave, Buck. I guess I'm a freak of nature. Some men are
born color blind. I was just for some reason born without the
emotion folks call fear. It was left out of my nature. I've
never felt afraid."

Buck's wool gathering was ended with the sudden trans-
formation from the spine jarring shocks of the Ford bouncing over the irregular ruts of the county dirt roads to the
rhythmic grinding noise of his tires as they climbed up on
the cobblestone brick paving of Logan Station. He began to
give thought to what he ought to say to Bud.

The Saddle Rock Hotel was a boarding hotel for
drummers working the Logan Station territory. It stood half
a block up the hill from the Santa Fe Depot, and when Buck
walked into the lobby Bud was sitting in a leather covered
armchair alongside a potted fern, staring out the hotel
front's plate glass window.

"How you feeling?" Buck asked.

"Frustrated," Bud answered, his dark face sullen.

Buck grunted and sat down in the chair beside him. It
was now close to 9:00 P.M. and the streets outside were almost deserted. An occasional passer-by headed to or from
the depot walked along the gaslighted street outside.

"I've been down at the office all day," young Bud said.
"Nothing going on there. Mighty quiet. No word at all on
Wiley Lester. I've been sitting here waiting for the nine
thirty-five passenger train to come in. Thought I'd watch the
drummers check in. Then go upstairs and go to bed. Big excitement!"

"How's your arm?" Buck asked.

Bud flexed it. "Sore but sound," he said. "Doc says he'll
probably take the stitches out tomorrow."

Buck studied his dusty boot toes.

"Well, Bud," he said, "we've got a chore to do. Hynote
ain't working out." Concisely, he told Bud the information
the afternoon and evening had turned up. "We're going to

have to go to Cimarron Bend and ask him to turn in his deputy's commission. You feel up to it?"

Bud Reed was already half out of his chair and grinning eagerly.

Buck advised, "Well now, settle back a minute." He went on patiently, "Here's the way we'll do it. We'll split up like we always do. I expect an argument. But when Hynote sees there are two of us, far enough apart that he can't get both of us, he'll tame down quick enough. I want to give him a chance to say his say. Bad as it looks, he may have some honest defense of what he's been up to. I want to give him a chance to talk, and hear him out."

Bud was standing now. "Where did you park that gulley-jumping hoopy of yours?" he asked impatiently.

VII

It was nearly midnight when they arrived in Cimarron Bend. Buck parked and they sat watching the steady procession of men ranging up and down the street. It was a reasonably quiet hour for the oilrush boomtown. Oilfield workers, up and ready to go to work on the midnight tower filled the street, but it was a sober crowd.

That would quickly change after midnight, when the off-work crowd came in to whoop it up for a while before turning in. At present, the swarm of men passing by were also passing up The Same Old Ikey's, a few entering to fortify themselves for the twelve hard hours of work ahead. Most were simply seeking out their ways of transportation from town out to the rigs where they worked.

It passed through Buck's mind that Barney Arles' Casino would probably be pretty deserted right now for the same reason. Even Etta's hurdy-gurdy girls who wandered about the street were being ignored. A shell-game artist who had set up his tray on the corner, inviting the roustabouts to get rich at his expense, was attracting no customers, wasting his spiel on the June night air.

Then Buck saw Hynote come out of The Same Old Ikey's and walk off, ferreting his way down the street through the orderly crowd in the opposite direction from where they sat.

"All right, Bud, there he is," Buck said quietly, watching Hynote's thin retreating back. "I'm going after him. You follow about thirty yards behind."

Buck flung a leg over the dummy door, hastened, then

drew up abruptly to fall in beside Hynote at the slow and easy pace at which the deputy was filtering his way through the foot traffic. Hynote's sharply cornering eyes caught Buck's presence immediately.

"Hell's fire! Buck!" he exclaimed. "What are you doing here? I figured you was long ago in bed with that purty young squaw of yours."

A flat-bed wagon pulled by four spans of draft mules and loaded with a pyramid of casing rolled up, slowing to stop alongside the curb ahead of them. Two waiting roughnecks started climbing up on the lazy board, ready to ride out to their rig.

Buck suggested, "Let's walk over to your room at the boarding house, Hynote."

"We're headed in the right direction," Hynote agreed. "But what for, Buck? You want to take another look at those slots I took away from Barney Arles? Or do you want another shot of Ikey's bad whiskey?" Hynote grinned.

Buck timed his answer carefully. As they approached the end of the pyramided wagonload of casing, he said, "No, Hynote. Barney Arles, Ikey Price, and Etta Redmond have all told me you're taking graft from them. A tool-pusher named Shaw told me this afternoon that you've put the arm on two of his workers for fifty bucks apiece. When we get to your room I want you to turn in your badge, and that deputy's commission I filled out and gave you."

Hynote's reaction was instantaneous. He drew and shot. But Buck had already stepped behind the load of casing, beyond the parked wagon's high wheel. Hynote's bullet went ricocheting. It whanged off the load of casing, leaving the long tubes of cast-iron pipe ringing like a struck bell.

As the bullet howled off into the night Buck opened his mouth to yell the words already framed in thought. YOU CAN'T WIN, HYNOTE—BUD IS COMING UP BEHIND YOU—but he was never able to utter them, for as the words formed in his throat Bud's .45 spoke.

The bullet struck Hynote in the left temple, slamming him headlong against the load of casing, from which he languidly slipped down, sinking to the ground to lie motionless in the gutter between board sidewalk and street. As the crowd gathered, encircling like buzzing flies, Bud Reed came elbowing his way through.

"He had already drawed and fired, Buck!" Bud declaimed. "He was going to kill you!"

Buck stood, staring numbly down at the dead man. "Not unless he could figure out some way to get a bullet through that load of iron casing," Buck said grimly. "You should have seen that, Bud. We had him whipsawed!"

The burned powder smell of Bud's spent cartridge hung in the still air, rising pungent and strong from the gun barrel of Bud's still-unholstered .45. Buck turned away.

"Put your gun away, Bud," he said. "It's done. Let's carry him down the street and load him in the car."

They carried Hynote's body to the car, doubling it with flexed knees, face against the black seat cushion, and Bud cranked the Ford. He ran then, hurrying around to climb in the open tonneau while Buck adjusted the throttle and choke.

"Where are we going?" Bud asked.

"Over to the pipe yard."

At the pipe yard Buck got out, grimly searched through the pockets of Hynote's clothing until he found Shaw's keys, and unlocked the toolhouse. There amid the usual doghouse litter of blocks and falls, coils of oil-soaked hemp line, tools and tongs, Shaw's two workmen were sound asleep on the shed's floor.

Buck toed them awake. "Okay, gents. Shaw said you're due on tower at midnight. We'll haul you out to the rig."

The driller and his tool-dresser got up sleepily, wandered out to the car and started to get in the back seat. The sight of Hynote's body there, with blood still leaking from the bullet hole in his left temple, brought the driller wide awake.

"Is that how you got us loose?" he asked in awe.

"That's how," Buck muttered.

"God almighty! I was mad as hell, but I wouldn't have killed him."

"Get on the running boards," Buck directed. "You're going to have to ride standing up."

They hauled the two crew members out to the lease for Shaw's graveyard shift, then with Hynote's body jouncing in the back seat, drove back to Logan Station.

Otto Dreyper's mortuary, in the intermingled area where a few of Logan Station's residences lapped into the edge of the town's business district, was an aged Victorian mansion, its lower floor converted to embalm bodies and hold services for the town's dead, its upstairs the living quarters of Dreyper's large and strangely death oriented family.

Otto, his horse-faced wife, and both his teen-age sons—all morticians by nature bent it seemed—were still asleep when Buck pulled the bell rope at the funeral parlor's front door. It was 4:00 A.M. Buck could hear the bell's peal echo in the farthest reaches of the house, and, presently, stairs creaked as someone approached the door.

It was opened by Otto himself, with his eldest son. Probably, they were accustomed to the arrival of business in the witching hours. Buck could recall hearing Otto Dreyper say, "It is our solemn responsibility to care for the remains of those who die at whatever hour the grim reaper beckons them to the beyond. Few choose the hour of their death."

Hyman Knote certainly hadn't chosen his, Buck reflected grimly. Otto and his son removed Hynote's body from the rear seat of the Ford with practiced ease, and gravity of countenance suiting the occasion. Rigor mortis had begun to set Hynote's body in the flexed and bent posture in which it had rested in the too short back seat.

Buck then drove around the square, turning west toward the Santa Fe tracks, dropped Bud off at the Saddle Rock, and steered his own way home. Undressing, pulling on his nightshirt, silently slipping into bed beside Kaahtidoah, Buck did not have the heart to awaken her and recount the night's tragedy.

As always, however soundly sleeping, she knew when he had come to her, and in this night when his own weariness and grievous regrets had obviated any need for her, she evidenced need for him. As Buck worked his body down between coverlet and sheet, his nightshirt, as usual, worked its way up to his armpits.

Before he could pull it down, Kaahtidoah slid over against him. He knew then that she had been dozing, anticipating his arrival, for even the flimsy nightie she customarily wore was gone. The silken texture of her flesh, soft and warming the hairy roughness of his chest and thighs, like a sudden refreshing gust, drove from his mind all remembrance of dead flesh and funereal thought.

Of an instant, Buck was utterly alive and tingling with the hard thrust of sudden desire. His blood coursed and his heart raced as, immersed in the softness of Kaahtidoah, the long and tenuous hour of pleasure sapped from spirit and body every tension, every worry and concern, replacing them with an utter euphoria that ended only when it easily transformed itself into deep, relaxing sleep.

As Kaahtidoah was not one to restrain, or withhold the pleasures of sex with coyness when they lay together, neither was she one to conceal or procrastinate when trouble loomed. She confronted life head on, with obdurate stubbornness, her philosophy being that problems were not solved with evasion or avoidance.

So she permitted Buck to arise late in the morning, shave, dress, and sit down to breakfast. But then, with the platter of eggs, bacon and biscuits she set before his steaming coffee, she presented him with the morning paper.

The headlines were boldface. Banks of subheads ranged beneath them to break the story and lead the reader into the columns of ten-point type that detailed the story.

DEPUTY KNOTE ASSASSINATED
SHERIFF CHARGED WITH GRAFT
Ministerial Alliance and Civic Betterment League
Demand Arraignment
of Sheriff Mather

As Buck read on his awe grew. Hynote, according to the Ministerial Alliance and Civic Betterment League, had instituted a "stern crackdown" on the joints and sin dens of Cimarron Bend, only to be assassinated by the sheriff and his "confederate" Bud Reed. According to flagrant charges by the Reverend Mark Jellico, president of the Logan Station Ministerial Alliance, Hynote had been no more than an "instrument" of the sheriff's.

If "Deputy Hyman Knote had truly been taking graft," as charged by some, he had been killed because Sheriff Mather feared Knote might eventually demand some portion of the illicit funds as his own share.

Buck put the paper down and looked across the table at Kaahti. She sat patiently awaiting his comment, one fist a chin rest beneath her darkly pretty face. A small light of unexpected amusement began to glint in her brown eyes as she correctly read the astonishment and shock in Buck's face.

Buck decided, mischievously, to give her no satisfaction. He let his glance fall from her high, rounded cheekbones to her perfectly rounded figure.

"Kaahti," he said, "I do believe you're gaining some weight."

"If you're as worried as you look," she said, her eyes measuring him, "you're going to lose some."

Buck knew her moods. She would never let her concern for him appear in a form so serious as to add to his own worries. Rather, she would try to persuade his spirits upward with a light approach and airy insouciance, though, inside, she was worried about him, knowing that his enthusiasm for a fight was waning just a little more with every passing year.

"What are you going to do?" she asked, and some of that inner seriousness had crept into her voice.

Buck folded the paper. "I'm going to ride downtown and get Bud," he said. "Then we'll pay a call on his honor Judge Caleb Hull." Buck went back into the bedroom to strap on his gun and don his leather vest. Carrying his slightly creased Carlsbad style sombrero in his hand, he paused in the kitchen to give Kaahti a sound good morning and good-bye kiss, walked on out to the barn, and saddled Chalky.

As invariably, it lifted his sagging spirits as soon as he stepped across the big stallion's saddle.

The ride into town had a reverse effect. Prior to that morning, it had never before really occurred to Buck how much he enjoyed the exchanges of greetings and the routine salutes from the folks who constituted his constituency in Logan Station. This ride was a silently reserved one. The hand waves and calls of "Good day, Sheriff" that always accompanied his passage were totally amiss this morning. Passers-by refused to meet his eyes. Glancing away, they scuttled on, or strode belligerently forward, depending on the spirit of their own make-up.

By the time Buck reached the town square he knew that his political popularity in Logan Station was at the lowest ebb it had yet reached in his public career. He was in this hour an outcast, being pointedly ignored. Reining Chalky right at the square, he rode to Talmadge's livery barn.

Dodging low in the saddle to avoid the lintel of Talmadge's double doorway, Buck drew rein and dismounted. Talmadge, halting and rheumatic, came up to take Chalky's reins and Buck passed comment on the chilly reception he was receiving around town this morning.

"Buck," Talmadge sulled irascibly, "you ought to know that these flatland town dudes are fickle. People are no damn good!"

Talmadge led Chalky away and Buck headed for the Saddle Rock Hotel. He met Bud coming along the sidewalk halfway there. As soon as their good mornings had been said, Bud's tentative and wary, Bud began expressing regrets.

"Buck, I sure am sorry," he apologized. "I tried to get a little sleep this morning, but all I could do was doze off for a little while, then wake up and think about what I had done to you. Hynote was your friend—"

"Some friend!" Buck interrupted. "Forget it, Bud. If I'd told you, before we started out on that errand, to be sure I had time to warn Hynote before you shot, you wouldn't have got caught in this wringer. But I didn't tell you. Let's forget it for a minute and get over here where we can talk, in private."

They were standing on the Gray Brothers' Bank corner, where every old-timer in town came to whittle and spit, and where a pair of them sat now, like ancient turkey buzzards, on the iron railing which separated the brick sidewalk from the stairway descending below street level to the basement of the bank building.

Both the old-timers were staining the sidewalk yellow with overflow from the generous cuds in their jaws. Both had their ears pointed at Buck's and Bud's conversation. The sheriff and his young deputy moved down the railing out of earshot. Leaning there, beside the red and white candy striped pole advertising the barbershop in the basement of the Gray Brothers' building, Bud asked confidentially, "Have you seen today's paper?"

"Kaahti made me a present of it when I sat down to breakfast this morning," Buck said grimly.

Resting their hips against the iron railing, silent and thoughtful, Buck broke the silence to ask, "Doc taken those stitches out of your arm yet?"

"That's where I was headed," Bud replied. "Up to his office."

"Well," Buck exhaled a long breath of resignation, "I think we've got a stop to make first."

"Where?"

"I expect we need to pay a call on Judge Hull in his chambers."

They crossed the city square to the Victorian front of the courthouse, so meant by the citizenry to be majestic with its broad entry accent. Any majesty that might have been implied by the elegance of its florid masonry was lost in the public building stench that overwhelmed their nostrils as they entered.

Continuing down the wide, wood-floored, and squeaking hallway, they climbed the stairway to the courtroom on the top floor. Judge Caleb Hull's court stood empty, dusky with shadows sharply contrasted to the bright June sunlight outside its multipaneled windows. The gaslight globes on each side of the judge's high bench were dark.

Buck circled the jury box, Bud following, and knocked on the door of Hull's chambers. The judge's bailiff, stooped and thin, macabre in his elbow-length black sleeve guards, bid them enter. Hull reared pompously back in the creaking swivel chair behind his desk, half-rising to greet them, then his pomposity took on a suddenly different aspect as he recognized who his visitors were.

Buck concluded that, while Hull's red face did not blanch exactly white, its ruddiness faded to a pale pink hue. When Buck drew his gun, Judge Caleb Hull started completely from his chair as if impelled to seek sanctuary, but Buck only reversed the weapon with a deft twirl, his finger in the trigger guard, and presented it, butt foremost, to the judge.

Buck then unclipped the badge from his vest, and laid it on Hull's desk, while motioning to Bud to do likewise. Caleb Hull recovered his composure, holding Buck's gun loosely in his fat hand.

"Sheriff Mather," he assured Buck grandiloquently, "you have saved us a time consuming effort in coming here voluntarily. I was on the point of dispatching my bailiff to search you out."

"Fine," Buck said noncommittally, as Bud's revolver and badge joined his on the desk. "Bud and I will consider ourselves relieved of duty until we get this thing worked out. When do we get our day in court?"

"That will come, all in due process," Judge Hull averred portentously. "Your preliminary arraignment is set on my docket for two o'clock tomorrow afternoon." The judge hauled out his turnip watch to consult it as closely as if the hearing was going to be within the hour.

Buck, his jaw muscles working in forbearance, utterly frustrated at the man's pompous-ass mannerisms, asked quietly, "What provision do you intend to make for law enforcement in this county, Judge, while the sheriff's office is vacant?"

"Don't concern yourself, Mr. Mather," Hull said. Buck felt he detected an unnecessary emphasis on the "mister."

Hull propounded, "A sterling and elemental example of law enforcement—the people themselves—will prevail in this crisis."

Buck stared at him fixedly, weighing this enigmatic statement.

"Well, your honor," he said, "you took an oath to uphold the law just the same as I did."

Buck turned on his boot heel to leave the office, pausing only to open the door and let Bud precede him out into the hallway.

Bud stopped there to wait for Buck, then, when Hull's door was closed, asked, "What are we going to do now, Buck?"

The suspended sheriff suggested, "Let's go fishing, Bud."

VIII

The Ford was loaded with cane poles. Buck drove, Kaahti in the middle wearing a split riding skirt, buckskin moccasins, and a loose fitting blouse of red-dyed gingham that enhanced her berry brown complexion like maple leaves in autumn. Bud, beside her, rode relaxed, his booted foot thrust out over the right hand door.

Buck steered the Ford over twin tracks almost lost in brush and undergrowth. This obscure trail through the blackjacks had probably remained unused since they had come over it to raid and shut down Jake Vandergriff's whiskey still almost six months ago.

Buck shut off the switch and the rattling flivver coasted to a halt near the edge of a crystal pool, behind which a moist red sandstone bluff rose high enough to darken the afternoon sun. Tricklets of silver water dripped and ran from the face of the moist bluff, running musically into the small pool.

It was the same spring fed pool that had supplied the water for the barrels of sour mash Vandergriff had distilled through the crude copper coil that Buck and Bud had confiscated when they had raided the moonshine still. A few staves and remnants of the barrels they had axed apart and broken up during the raid still lay around the spring.

"I've been wanting to try this place ever since we put friend Jake out of business," Buck confided in anticipation.

Bud slid out over the door and went to peer down into the

water. "Buck," he said eagerly, "there is perch in there as big as the palm of my hand!"

The noisy approach of the Ford had silenced the timber, but now Bud's voice, restrained and quiet in these surroundings, seemed to reassure the cross-timbers' wildlife. A crow, wheeling overhead, announced their presence, somewhat raucously, apparently conveying the intelligence that they were unarmed with shotguns or rifles, for a bushy tailed squirrel came scurrying down out of a walnut tree to resume his search among the rustling leaves for last fall's abundance of nuts.

A dove called from far off through the timber, and its mate replied from its concealment high in a giant cedar, grown to immensity from the plenitude of water beneath its spring fed roots and the luxuriant fertility of the leaf mulched timber floor.

"You got the frying pan, Kaahti," Buck prompted, "and plenty of salt and pepper?"

"You bet," she chirped agreeably, "and dough for fry bread, potatoes to hash brown, beans to bake, a sack of apples, and some of those peanut butter cookies I baked day before yesterday."

Buck got out. "I'll build you a fire."

"You'll build an Indian girl a fire?" she chided. "My grandmothers were building fires to cook their men's meat while your cavemen ancestors were still eating it raw!"

Buck shrugged and grinned. "I'd sure rather fish anyhow." He started untying the cane poles.

By the time he and Bud had set the floats on half a dozen lines to proper depth and baited the' hooks, Kaahti had a small and totally smokeless cooking fire going. She came to join them.

Bud offered her a cane pole, but Buck said, "Kiowas were never much for eating fish, Bud. The turtle is the totem of one of Kaahti's clans and the old elders will tell you it's as risky to eat anything out of the water as it is to eat bear meat."

"I'm not so old fashioned," she said. "Let me try."

She moved down toward the end of the pool, where the clear water eddied out to form a stream running off toward the Cimarron. She caught not only the first fish, but four of the seven that Buck dressed for supper.

All three pitched in on the cooking chores, Bud peeling potatoes, Buck frying fish, Kaahti concocting the mixture of fried bacon, molasses, mustard, and onions with which to bake the beans, then adding hickory branches to the fire to give the fried perch and baked beans a properly smoky flavor.

Bud had insisted on bringing a tarpaulin, but the shade here by the spring was so dense there was no need to rig it overhead. So they spread it out by the fire for sitting on. On it they sat, taking turns at the occasional needs of fire tending, stirring, or turning, the cooking viands. Without talk, they listened to the conversation of the woods. The breeze soughing in the branches of the tall cedars replied to the rustling leaves of the deciduous trees, the oaks, hickorys, walnuts, and maples, that gave way gradually over rising terrain to the tangled blackjacks of the cross-timbers country.

From the higher meadows came the bright, twisting cries of the meadowlark. Nearer, the peter bird kept up its persistent complaint. As evening came on a mocking bird began skylarking from the highest branches of a cottonwood, imitating them all.

They ate their supper hungrily, commenting only on its deliciousness, with never a word about the Logan Station-Cimarron Bend turmoil they had left behind, purposely avoiding any such reminders of the disagreeable. After supper, the dishes and utensils washed and packed, they loafed again on the spread tarpaulin, watching the last vermilion rays of the sun give way to dusk.

Calling bobwhite quail and the lament of a rain crow anticipated the nightfall, and with the descent of full darkness the timber fell silent for a time. With the dying of the last strength of the day's wind, they watched the evening star appear in the western sky. The Pleiades came fading in to keep bright Venus company, and as the myriad of stars increased and brightened, the melancholy hooting of a great horned owl reminded them that it was getting late. They loaded up and drove back to Logan Station.

Driving through town for the purpose of dropping Bud off at the Saddle Rock Hotel, Kaahti commented on the thickening crowd as they approached the town square. It was not Saturday night. It was Wednesday night and all the stores were closed. With a widening range of generalities they continued to speculate on the number of people out and about as they approached the square.

Buck diverted his attention from his driving long enough for a quick glance at his watch. "It's after nine o'clock," he said in amazement. Nine o'clock was generally going-to-bed time for most of Logan Station's population.

A block this side of the square it became apparent that they were not going to be able to drive through. The street was choked with parked vehicles and foot traffic heading for the square. The square itself was lined with people, standing and waiting, as spectators stand and wait in anticipation of the coming of a parade.

Buck parked the Ford. "Let's get out and go have a look, Bud," he suggested curiously.

Together, they walked the intervening half block, leaving Kaahti alone in the car. Buck and Bud joined the line of quietly waiting spectators along the east side of the square. They had arrived just in time to see the approach of the first riders.

Buck understood at a glance, for the approaching riders were masked. A lone man on horseback led the procession, followed by pairs and threes that strung out behind him for the better part of a block. Each of the riders in the procession, like their ominously foreboding leader, wore the tall, peaked, white hood of the Ku Klux Klan. Each was completely draped, from shoulder to heels in the Klan's loose-fitting white robe.

Even the horses they rode were hooded and masked; from heads across withers, saddle and haunches, each horse's white muslin robe fell almost to its fetlocks. It was patently impossible to recognize a single one of the men, or any of the horses in the oncoming congregation.

Each man carried, high above his head, a fiery cross of pitch pine that burned smokily. The crowd watched in smothered silence. Occasionally a wide-eyed youngster would cry out in emotional excitement from a surge of inquietude incited by the apparitions riding past. Only the clip-clop of ironshod hoofs on cobblestone brick pavement relieved the strained silence.

Even to Buck, the approaching horses of the spooky parade, with hooded and masked men astride their backs, seemed immense and spectral.

He said softly, to Bud, "Good god! This is what Hull meant by 'the people themselves.' They aim to take the law in their own hands."

Bud nodded. "This Ku Klux outfit is the bunch that will be enforcing it. Whatever parts they choose to enforce—"

Buck felt almost as if he was back in Johnson County. This time not as one of the "enforcers" but on the other side —one of those the force was most likely to be used against.

Bud was castigating himself again. "It's my fault, Buck," he said. "If I hadn't been so all fired quick-triggered, Hynote would be alive, and we wouldn't have this bunch of spooks coming at us!"

Buck shook his head calmly. "No, Bud. This thing has been a long time a-planning. These jaybirds have been rigging themselves out, having their wives cut up the bed-sheets and sew up these ghost robes, and having secret

meetings for a long time. Bound to have. It takes a while for
any vigilante outfit to plan a takeover, then screw up the
nerve to do it. If it hadn't been for Hynote's killing, they'd
of found some other excuse. I'll bet this parade has been in
the making for weeks. It's a wonder we haven't heard some
pieces of gossip ourselves. It was already well enough
known that they could spread the alarm all over town by
word of mouth while we were out fishing this afternoon.
They got the word out that tonight was the night of the big
Ku Klux parade without us knowing it. They've been watching us pretty close, Bud. They knew we were out of town.
You can be mighty sure of that."

One of the masked riders turned, making a feinted charge
at the edge of the crowd, where Buck and Bud stood. Neither of them gave way, but a small boy, held in his mother's
arms to watch the parade, was terrorized by the sudden approach of the white phantom. The small boy panicked,
screaming hysterically. Bud charged out through the fringe
of the crowd to fling his arms up in the face of the horse.

The word he shouted—"Boo!"—brought a small titter of
appreciation from a few of the crowd, but it was clear that
most of the spectators were as overawed by the solemn
threat of the parading Ku Klux as the child had been.

As Bud retraced his steps through the crowd edge, he
suddenly exclaimed, "Look yonder, Buck!"

Turning his attention where Bud had pointed, Buck saw
an old man hurling a rock toward the ending parade of
masked riders. The rock he threw struck the flank of one of
the passing horses and the startled beast almost bolted into
the crowd on the far side of the street before its struggling
masked rider could bring it under control.

The Ku Klux member fighting his bolting horse lost his
fiery cross and it fell to the brick street to shatter in a
shower of sparks. The old man had his arm cocked to throw
another rock when Buck and Bud closed in on him. Buck

grabbed the upraised arm, deflecting its missile, as Bud circled to the old man's far side.

Together they quietly eased the wild-eyed rock thrower
back out of the crowd and against the plate glass show window of The Dixie Store behind him. The old man was
mouthing obscenities, a trickle of saliva running from the
corner of his hate-wrenched mouth. Beside himself with
fury, he wrenched and twisted, attempting to break away,
demanding, "Turn me a-loost!"

"Now, settle down, mister," Buck urged.

The attention of the crowd was so transfixed by the passing departure of the hooded Ku Klux, and the remains of the
fallen cross still burning in the street, as to take no notice of
the struggle going on against the store front window behind
them.

"Settle down, mister," Buck urged again.

"You danged old fool," Bud started angrily. "You hit one
of them horses, and it could have bolted into the crowd and
hurt somebody. Maybe killed some kid. There's a lot of
women with babies in their arms over there!"

The old man settled back almost immediately. "Never
thought of that," he admitted. Some of the wild look went
out of his eyes, but the anger, the fury of undiluted hatred,
remained.

"The Ku Klux never thought of that, either," Buck commented agreeably, further calming him, then fully releasing
his hold on the old man's arm.

"That's right," came the hard mouthed response. "They
never think of nothin' but hurtin' somebody. That's all they
thought of the night they strapped my boy, and whipped
him. Beat him to death!"

"Where was this?" Buck asked.

"Down in the delta country," the old man answered.
"Scared my boy's wife so she had a miscarriage. They didn't
think nothin' about that, either! They don't mind killin' babies!"

"I expect maybe they don't," Buck still agreed gently, "but the delta country is a long ways from here, mister. It couldn't have been the same Ku Klux as this bunch."

"One Ku Kluxer is like any other," the old man declared furiously. "Git 'em hid under them sheets an' you cain't tell one from another'n."

"What were they after your boy for?" Bud asked inquisitively.

The parade of hooded riders had disappeared around the far corner, turning away from the square, and the crowd began to break up gradually, talking excitedly as they dispersed, paying no attention to Buck, Bud, and the old man.

"Claimed his wife was part nigger," the old man said. "She ain't. But what difference would it have made if she was?" He studied Bud intently in the light of the gas streetlamp beneath which they stood. "She's whiter'n you are."

"My maw always said our family was part Choctaw," Bud said.

"My boy's wife was part Seminole," said the old man, "but what the hell difference does that make? Is that any reason to strap a man down and whip him with a wire rope? It killed my boy. Even split his private parts wide open."

Buck stared at the old man, then looked down at the sidewalk shaking his head in sympathy and disgust. He offered his hand.

"Mister, I'm Sheriff Buck Mather, and this is my deputy, Bud Reed."

"You mean you *was* the sheriff, and this *was* your deputy," the old gent prompted. "Mather, that Klan outfit aims that you won't ever be able to call yourself 'Sheriff' anymore. They aim to throw you out of office." He paused, as if ruminating on the truth and gravity of his own speech, then extended his own hand. "I'm J. B. Wells," he said, "and I apologize for being cantankerous and an old know-it-all. Maybe you can whip the bastards."

Bud shook hands in turn. "You ain't telling us anything

we didn't already know," he said, again turning bellicose. "They threw us out all right."

"Once you're out," Buck added, "it's sure no easy trick getting back in."

Wells studied him. "Don't give in to that bunch without tryin'," he urged, "and if you need any help from a wore out old man, don't hesitate to call on me."

As Wells stumped off, Buck and Bud turned to mosey back to the car. The parade having broken up, there were only a few Klansmen in sight, apparently having disbanded to ride to their homes, but as Buck and Bud rounded the corner toward the car, two of the hooded Klansmen were approaching it from the rear.

The two Ku Klux had apparently circled around through the alley and were almost alongside the Ford in which Kaahti sat alone. Buck hastened his pace, falling into a fast trot. One of the Klansmen rode past the car, but the other, still carrying his burning cross, leaned to look inside it.

He lowered the fiery cross then, to let its baleful light flicker across Kaahti's face. Buck heard him yell something toward his companion about "Buck Mather's squaw," and the other Ku Klux turned his horse back.

Buck approached the Klansman leaning into the car and grabbed his white-robed arm. The burning cross fell as Buck pulled the man off his horse. The other Klansman, seeing his buddy in trouble, spurred momentarily toward him, then had a change of heart. He spun, turning his horse's tail toward his buddy and fled amid the noisy clatter of his horse's iron shod hoofs. Bud Reed took after him, running hard in hot pursuit.

The rider Buck had jerked from his horse crouched now beside the flaring remains of his pine torch cross. His hood had fallen away and Buck recognized him—a ferret faced clerk from Petty's Racket Store, whose name Buck could not at the moment recall. The fallen store clerk shouted a threat,

garbled and unintelligible with fright, then he scuttled off
down the alley.

His horse, masked in its muslin robe, stood, indecisive, for
a moment, then startled by Buck's upflung arms, went clat-
tering off down the alley following its owner. Bud came
moping back out of the opposite alleyway, across the street.

"No chance with him on horseback and me afoot," he
said. "He got away."

Buck had pulled off his hat and stood beside the car
scratching his head. "Bud, who is that mealy-mouthed
sucker who sells pots and pans down at Petty's Racket
Store?"

"You mean Jesse Renan?" Bud asked.

"The one who's always wiping his sweaty palms on his
britches and bowing and scraping till hell won't have him—"

"That's him," Bud agreed.

"That's the fellow who was under that Ku Klux hood—the
one I just pulled off his horse."

Bud's mouth hung agape with surprise.

"He's the kind," Buck said, "who can get mean as a snake
when he's got something to hide under."

"We ought to hunt him up in the morning," Bud
suggested.

"Well," Buck pondered, "we'll see. Get in, Bud. We'll
take you on over to the hotel."

"Heck no, Buck. I can walk on over to my place from
here. You and Kaahti go on home and turn in."

Kaahti offered, somewhat timorously, from the inside of
the car, "It appears to me it's time both of you got at least
one decent night's sleep. Like common, everyday working
folks."

"Or maybeso like a respected member of the Ku Klux
Klan." Buck grinned. He went to crank the Ford and, as
Bud cut off across the courthouse square, Buck ran to swing
his leg across the dummy door. Climbing in, he backed the

car into the alley down which the Klansman had retreated and turned it toward home.

Buck kept to the side streets between the center of town and their house, thinking he might spot another Klan member or so riding into their own yards and, by knowing where they lived, later identify them. But he saw no one.

As he and Kaahti neared their own home, approaching it down a cross street from the northwest, Buck could see reflected flames guttering across their front porch. At first he thought their house was on fire. His boot toe mashed down the accelerator and the Ford hoopy was careening at a precarious speed as they came around the final corner fronting their house.

The house was not burning. It was a fiery cross stobbed down in the front yard, halfway between the brick sidewalk and the house. It had been burning there quite awhile and was more than three fourths consumed. Its flames were beginning to sputter and die on the charred wood. Buck got out, walked over to it, kicked it down, and stamped it out.

They went inside to undress for bed, Kaahti clearly apprehensive. Buck talked steadily, reassuringly, and kiddingly remarked that it was the earliest he had managed to turn in within recent memory. But before blowing out the lamp, and making no comment as he did so, he removed his twelve-gauge shotgun from the case where it stood in the corner of his wardrobe cabinet, put it together, checked to see that both barrels were loaded, and stood it against the wall between his pillow and the iron bedstead.

Then, undisturbed by any emotion even remotely apprehensive, Buck Mather went promptly to sleep and slept soundly until he was awakened by the pounding on the front door. He was sharply alert then in an instant, but lay very still. It was pitch dark.

Kaahti, beside him, said softly, "Buck?"

He touched her hand gently then slid out of bed. Taking up the shotgun he stepped to the window. Cracking open the drapes for a covert peek, Buck noted that it was that darkest dark that precedes the dawn. He would have guessed that it was a little after 4:00 A.M. The pounding on the front door commenced again, and he went toward the parlor.

From the bay window projecting out from the living room, onto the porch, he could hazily see, and study, a human figure. It was a shape of even darker dark, silhouetted against the blackness of the night and the pale white of the house's painted slabboard siding. It was a man, leaning with one hand and forearm against the doorjamb. He pounded the screen molding with his other fist.

The shape of him, and the attitude of his stance, at last made the man identifiable to Buck. It was Barney Arles.

Buck once more scanned all he could see of the front yard and the darkened street beyond. Arles seemed to be alone. A horsedrawn buggy, in which Arles must have come, stood in the front yard. Buck stopped to open the door. The shotgun gripped and ready in his right hand, he slid the door's bolt with his left, and reached to turn the knob.

With the door open, even the night's dark could not conceal Arles' condition as he leaned there outside the screen door. His clothing hung, torn almost off his body. His face was streaked with blood. He leaned, barely able to stand.

Buck breathed, "Good god, man!" and opened the screen door.

IX

"They hit us at 2:00 A.M., Buck," Arles gasped.

"Who hit you?"

"The Ku Klux."

Buck thought it through. Yes, they would just about have had time. The parade had disbanded a little before ten. His thought that the Klan members, after disbanding, would head for their homes had been in error. They must have formed up somewhere outside of town, and ridden straight for Cimarron Bend. So they would have arrived there about 2:00 A.M.

"Come in here, Barney," Buck said. "Shut the door behind you. Anybody besides you hurt?"

"Anybody besides me—good lord, Buck!" Arles was obviously still in shock. "My place is wiped out. Burned to the ground. They stripped my croupier, my dice man, and both my dealers to the waist, whipped them with a cat-o'-nine-tails, and drove them out of town. Ikey Price's place is gutted. They didn't dare set it on fire. Being where it is it would have burned the whole damn town down. They tarred and feathered Ikey."

"What about Etta Redmond?" Buck asked grimly.

"Etta is dead."

Buck leaned the shotgun against the wall, and sat down on the couch.

"I don't believe they meant to kill her," Arles said. "I'll give them that. But there was a lot of wild shooting, like there always is in a vigilante raid. I think Etta just got in the way of a stray bullet."

"Stray bullet, hell!" Buck Mather exploded. "She got in front of the gun of some son-of-a-bitch who had been patronizing her house and wanted to make sure his wife back home would never find out."

For a moment Buck sat with his face buried in his hands, then he stood up. "Here, Barney, lay down on this couch. I'll get Kaahti—"

"No, no, Buck! I can't stay here. I'm sure two or three of the Ku Klux are still on my trail. If they catch up with me I'll get the tar and feathers, just like Ikey did."

"Where is Ikey now?"

"God only knows. They hit Etta's place first. Scattered her girls through the timber like a covey of quail. Etta's getting killed tamed them down for just a little while. But by the time they'd tore Ikey's place up they were out for blood again. We'd had a little warning at the Casino and locked up tight. It didn't even slow 'em down. Us being out on the edge of town like we were they just set fire to my place and burned us out. But they never caught me. I got cut up and hurt breaking out the window of my place to get away from the fire. I don't know whose buggy that is I'm driving, so I guess I'm a horse thief now, too. I just wanted to stop here long enough to file a complaint—"

"Against who?" Buck asked forlornly.

"Hell, I don't know! The Ku Klux Klan! A gang of John Does!"

"Well, it wouldn't do any good if you did know who, Barney," Buck said. "I turned in my badge and gun yesterday. They're going to arraign me on charges of graft and corruption at two o'clock this afternoon."

Arles stood stunned. "I'd better get out of here then," he said. "I'm not doing myself any good, and if they catch up with me here they'll just burn your house down like they did my place."

Barney Arles pulled open the front door, looked out hastily, and ran. The morning star was above the horizon now. Daylight was beginning to brighten. The last Buck saw of Arles he was driving the buggy away, lashing the horse up to increase its speed as it fled down the street.

There was really nothing else to do—Buck went back to bed.

But he could not stay there.

He could not go to sleep. He knew that Kaahti lay wide awake beside him, taut and curious. It awed him that, in her strong self-discipline, she could not have arisen to eavesdrop —even on her own husband.

Her steady faith and confidence in him helped Buck to decide what he had to do, so he said to her, softly, "All right, let's get up and fix some breakfast."

While they ate, he repeated to her what had happened in Cimarron Bend. Then he went to the stable, saddled Chalky, and rode downtown. He tied the big stallion to the courthouse hitch rail, then leaned against the rail momentarily, watching John Barnhouse directing the light morning traffic in the street where Logan Station Avenue intersected the courthouse square.

A pair of loafers stood on the opposite corner, grimacing, aping Barnhouse, making filthy finger gestures, and yelling sidewalk comedian witticisms at him. They were laughing uproariously at their own antics and wisecracks. Buck turned away in disgust and climbed the courthouse steps.

He knocked on the door of the judge's chambers. Hull answered his knock and it occurred to Buck that a man had to credit the old goat with being willing to follow his own early-to-rise and early-to-work precepts. Buck opened the door.

The judge offered no word of welcome, nor did he invite Buck to come in and sit down. He sat pompously at his desk staring snuffily at the suspended sheriff.

"Judge," Buck began. "The Ku Klux raided Cimarron Bend last night."

"Humph!"

"They destroyed a lot of property out there," Buck went on.

"There was some property out there that needed destroying," Hull declared.

"A woman got killed in the fracas," Buck added.

"That iniquitous community of anarchy has had its man for breakfast almost daily for weeks." Hull was obdurate. "Perhaps they decided it was time for a little variety."

Hull's arrogant callousness stunned Buck. "Do you hear what I'm telling you?" he asked. "We're talking about riot and murder!"

"The situation in Cimarron Bend required bitter medicine," Hull countered.

"You can't be serious." Buck's lantern jaw clamped shut grimly.

"The people's will be done," Hull intoned in piety.

"Hull, what you're warranting here, and even commending, violates territorial law."

"When you address me, sir, you will use my official title, Judge Hull or 'Your Honor!' Otherwise you risk being cited for contempt. There is no law against the Ku Klux Klan in this territory."

"There is a vigilante law which forbids unauthorized posses," Buck said thinly. "I'm asking you for reinstatement as sheriff of this county to deal with an emergency."

"Mather, you are a discredited public official. I will have no more truck with you. Leave my office at once. I'll deal with you at your arraignment this afternoon."

Buck stood in the doorway, wrestling to maintain his composure, fighting down his fury. He gave up the fight then, stepping back outside the doorway. He slammed the door shut behind him, and descended the staircase. Striding through the downstairs hallway, he burst through the courthouse front doors so precipitously that he barely avoided a collision with Shorty Long.

Shorty had himself been coming up the portico steps under a considerable head of steam. He halted abruptly to exclaim, "I'm sure glad to find you, Buck. Fellow down the street said he thought he seen you ride up here, and I seen Chalky tied up at the hitch rail. We need help bad!"

"You're not likely to get much from a discredited public official—"

"Now, Buck, don't get huffy," Shorty urged. "I know how you feel, but John Barnhouse has gone berserk."

Buck waited, still struggling to bring his surging impatience under control.

Shorty said, "A couple fellows were hoorawing him this morning. That got it started. The crowd helling him growed, and the hoorawing got worse, until John finally just got a belly full. He got his hands on a shotgun somewhere and he's holed up in the stairwell over by lawyer Wooley's office. There's a pretty good-sized crowd down there now trying to screw up their nerve to go upstairs after him. If they do, somebody could get killed, and it could be John hisself."

Buck thought it over. He had known John Barnhouse since his first arrival in Logan Station. The big, rawboned, simple man's mind had failed to mature beyond five or six years of age, and he had never lost his small boy desire to be a policeman.

With his toy billy club, policeman's hat, and cap pistol, his occasional spells of directing traffic had become an accepted fixture in the routine of Logan Station's folkways. Tolerated by everyone, it was accepted by most, but there were a few town smart alecks who could not resist the temptation to tease and bullyrag this strange middle-aged man they knew as "the town halfwit."

Left alone, Barnhouse usually soon tired of directing traffic and went on to other amusements. But Buck, in the back of his mind, had always known that danger existed in the situation. Barnhouse had a potential for violence. Buck certainly felt that his failure to recognize what his subconscious had been telling him for so long a time involved an obligation here from which he could not turn aside.

"Well, hell—" he muttered.

"All that hoorawing finally got to him, Buck," Shorty pleaded. "He has gone plumb crazy."

"All right, Shorty," Buck agreed. "Let's go."

They crossed the courthouse lawn, bending left around the square. As soon as their passage around the portico of that ornate Victorian building had opened enough for them to see beyond the stairs and scrolled columns that had obscured their view, Buck could see the crowd milling in the street at the foot of lawyer Wooley's office stairway.

Most of the onlookers were standing well back out of the way but a few meandered carelessly around in front of the darkened maw where the stairwell ascended up into the office building. As Buck and Shorty reached the curb, one of the young men, overeager to demonstrate his bravery, feinted a charge up the stairway. That he had no intention of entering was apparent in his circling run, but he hooted a taunt up the stairway as he passed it.

"You're yellow, John," he howled. "You ain't got the guts to come down here!"

The shouted taunt precipitated a booming, echoing, shotgun blast from the inside upper level of the stairway. Shotgun pellets ripped splinters of wood from the overhead beam of the stairway entrance. Pellets of shot and splinters hurtled out over the heads of the crowd.

The taunter sped away. His hat, caught either by the pellet spray or the speed of the taunter's running, went flying off as he swung out into the street.

Buck stepped without pausing to the stairway entrance. Staring up into the darkness, black in contrast to the bright sunlight of the street, he called out:

"Take it easy, John. It's the chief. I'm coming up."

Unarmed, his hands in plain view, swinging easily at his sides to balance his ascending, Buck methodically climbed to the first landing. He spotted John and his shotgun then. The rawboned Barnhouse was plastered flat against the wall beside a closed door, alongside the banister at the head of the stairs. Gilt lettering on the door's opaque glass announced "*A. Wooley, Attorney-at-Law.*" Buck went on relentlessly, to the stairhead, and turned to face Barnhouse.

"That's enough now, John," he said. "I'll take the shotgun."

Barnhouse saluted hesitantly. "Sure, Chief. I was trying to keep 'em from raiding the jail and turning the prisoners loose."

"You've done fine, John," Buck assured him and put his hand on the shotgun.

Barnhouse released it. Buck put his arm around the awkwardly built man's shoulders. Barnhouse was as tall as Buck and as powerfully built. They walked down the stairway, together.

As they emerged, coming out on the sidewalk, Buck said, "You've been working overtime, John. It's past time for you to go off duty."

"I know, Chief, but this is a ugly mob. Maybe I prevented a lynching."

Buck nodded solemnly. "Go home and get some sleep now, John."

"All right, Chief," Barnhouse saluted and ambled off down the street.

The thirtyish, dudishly dressed smart aleck who had lost his hat in the shotgun blast stepped out into the street to retrieve his headgear, then came to accost Buck.

"By god he ought to be arrested and jailed!" he charged peevishly.

Buck glared him down. "I can't even arrest the ones who ought to be in jail. I'm suspended. Go see his honor the county judge."

As Buck turned away from the petulant and brazen persecutor of John Barnhouse, J. B. Wells came sidling up to him. The aged rock thrower from the Ku Klux Klan parade of the previous night spoke quietly, surreptitiously, from the corner of his mouth as he walked past Buck.

"Tonight midnight. Red Jaggers' pasture," Wells murmured hoarsely.

Uncomprehending, Buck reached for Wells' shoulder to ask the old gentleman to repeat, when he spotted an incident taking place across the square which drew his full attention. A man was backing out of The Owl Drug Store.

Something about his attitude alerted Buck's instincts. He saw the handkerchief knot at the nape of the man's neck then and Buck knew what had alerted him. The man's back and the attitude in which he was standing suggested that he was holding a pistol pointed at the drug store's front doors. His forearm was upraised, and concealed by his body.

There was something else—

Buck mused, watching the man pull down the handkerchief that had been hiding his face. The fellow turned and hurried into the Floradora Pool Hall next door to the drug store. He was slipping the pistol into his pants pocket, and with a glimpse of his profile, Buck recognized him instantly. Wiley Lester had surfaced.

Buck set out across the square at a run and was shoving his way through the Floradora's batwing screen doors before the thought again struck him that he could make no arrest, of Wiley Lester or anyone else, regardless of what they had done.

But curiosity held and impelled him. Buck scanned the sparse crowd populating the pool hall, then he wandered casually back through the place. Halfway back a teen-age rack boy, leaning over a billiard table, was racking up the balls. Buck stopped beside one of the gentlemen players who stood chalking his cue.

Touching the rack boy on his back, Buck asked, "Tall

fellow with a black silk bandanna around his neck hind-side-before come through here a few minutes ago?"

"Sure did, Sheriff," the boy nodded. "Hawk nosed gent, needed a shave. Had his lips kind of stretched back like he might be grinning, but he wasn't. He was just showing his teeth."

Buck did grin. "You saw more than I did, son. That must have been him. Where is he? In the toilet?"

"Huh-uh," the rack boy shook his head. "He went straight through. Came in the front door. Went out the back door."

Buck went on back and out into the alley. No human in sight in any direction. The deposed sheriff lost his eagerness for a chase he could not consummate with an arrest. But he could not help but brood on it. Wiley Lester certainly had a spectral penchant for sudden appearances, then rapid, equally sudden, and almost ghostly, disappearances.

Buck turned left and entered the back door of The Owl Drug Store. Making his way up through the rear of the pharmacy among shelves laden with pharmaceuticals and supplies, he caught sight of the eldest of the two brothers who, in partnership, operated the store.

Seth Ray, bent with arthritis and nearly hunchbacked, had tossed aside his pharmacist's black alpaca jacket and was thrusting his arms through the sleeves of his suit coat as he headed for the front door.

"Seth!" Buck called out.

The pharmacist turned. "Sheriff! We just tried to telephone you. There's no one in your office! We've been held up—robbed. The bandit is not five minutes gone. He struck my brother. Asa is lying on a cot back there by the prescription counter. . . . I thought I'd go up to Judge Hull's office . . ."

"Here, I'll go with you," Buck offered.

In Judge Hull's office the elderly pharmacist opened the conversation pointedly.

"Judge Hull," Seth Ray began determinedly, "Asa and I have just been robbed."

Buck listened, sensing that Ray intended to guide this conversation in some direction he had been planning all the way up here. Judge Hull promptly launched into a familiar harangue.

"It is a deep disgrace," he said. "The depths to which law enforcement in this county has fallen is disreputable! We must all strive to work together toward—"

Seth Ray interrupted. Small and hunched, Ray cut in with the determined asperity of a wasp on course and boring in to sting.

"Perhaps we would not be having this flood of crime," he said, "if you had not deposed Sheriff Mather."

Caleb Hull altered his direction. "One robbing is hardly a 'flood of crime,' Mr. Ray.

"Your brother Asa," Hull went on, "is a member of the Civic Betterment League, which voted to suspend Mather—"

Ray again interrupted. "The vote was not unanimous, Caleb, as you well know. Asa was one of those who voted *against* requesting the sheriff's suspension."

Judge Hull glanced meaningfully at the flag which hung limp from its standard beside his desk. "In a democracy," he said, "the majority must rule."

"Even when it is controlled by a minority?"

"What do you mean?" Hull's chin came up, he was incensed.

"I mean, Caleb, that I do not believe a majority of the people in Logan Station will support your removal of Sheriff Mather. Those who oppose him are, for the most part, those who have been arrested by him, some others who resent being restricted by law, and a yet larger group of overpious bluenoses who are either short-sighted, or not too intelligent. Thinking people, Caleb, are not going to be in accord with what you have done, or the kind of mob violence that swept through Cimarron Bend last night."

"A jury of Mather's peers will finally decide that, you know, pharmacist Ray."

"I am even doubtful that you can empanel a jury of fair-minded people who will require Sheriff Mather's expulsion from office. Unless undue influence is used—"

Hull began aggressively, "Undue influence by—" and paused. Buck knew Caleb Hull had been at the point of demanding "by who?" but the judge again reversed his direction.

"If you have evidence to offer at the arraignment, Mr. Ray," Hull said, "I urge you to be here this afternoon to present it. Now, I have much work to do in preparation for the hearing and I must ask you to excuse me, gentlemen."

Buck assumed the "gentlemen" included him, since only he and Seth were in the office, and he left the office with a feeling of encouragement. At the foot of the stairs, Buck thanked Ray and parted company with him, the arthritic little pharmacist to return to his drug store, Buck continuing to Talmadge's livery to secure Chalky for the ride home.

As he rode Chalky through the noon hour streets, peopled with store clerks and office workers on their way to or returning from midday dinner, J. B. Wells' cryptic *midnight tonight, Red Jaggers' pasture* came to mind, and Buck kept an eye out for Wells, intending to ask him to clarify. He did not see him. Buck decided to ask Bud to hunt the old gent up before day was done, to determine what message Wells was intending to convey.

The thought that the Ku Klux might harass John Barnhouse passed through Buck's mind. As unlikely as it seemed that grown men would undertake to persecute the simple-minded Barnhouse, Buck knew there was no way of ascertaining who was beneath all those cone-shaped white hoods. The fellow who had been John's chief heckler at the stairway, who had demanded that Buck ought to arrest and jail him, might own a Klan hood and he might drag Barnhouse to a Klan meeting to redeem his own wounded pride. But

Wells had made his statement too soon after the Barnhouse
incident for the old gent to have knowledge of any intent of
the Klan to harass Barnhouse for going berserk. Wells had
to be referring to something else.

Buck put Chalky in the stable, unsaddled him, gunny-
sacked Chalky's sweaty back, fed him, and went in to eat his
own dinner.

BUCK

Buck was a federal fugitive but soon after the Barnettes
baked it in, he told them to leave town and keep him posted on
the cattle sale. Somebody for going there to Walls had
to be on hand watching the ————

Red and Chalky, in the ————— taught a little canopy
grazed Chalky on the side and hid himself comfortably in
the timber.

X

Since Kaahti absolutely and positively insisted on going to
the arraignment with him, Buck backed the Ford out of the
barn after dinner. He was always amused at Chalky's dis-
dainful reaction to the exhaust popping, and the stinking
blue cloud of acrid smoke it produced. Buck watched the
big white horse snort, toss his head angrily, and stamp the
straw litter in his stall as the Ford made its way in reverse,
protesting and jerky, down the barn's center runway over
the splintered old boards and into the alley.

Buck drove around in front of the house. Kaahti came out
dressed in a full, flowered blouse with a wide circular neck-
line loosely gathered around her shoulders and throat. She
wore an ankle length, brightly tinted dirndl skirt with a
flounce around the bottom, and, in her dark, smoothly
combed and braided brunette hair, a Caddo butterfly orna-
ment. Her self-crocheted, silken rebozo shawl lay about her
shoulders, and she looked more like a ceremonially dressed
young Indian matron going to an intertribal powwow than a
worried housewife on the way to stand by her husband during his sternest ordeal in court.

Buck grinned. He felt better. More optimistic than he had
been since the night he and Bud had so smoothly and
efficiently first captured Wiley Lester.

When they arrived in Judge Caleb Hull's courtroom they
found it overflowing. For the most part with interested spectators, but Buck was well pleased to see both Seth and Asa
Ray sitting among them. He wondered who was keeping The
Owl Drug Store open.

The Reverend Mark Jellico sat just behind the courtroom railing, in front of which County Attorney Marley Peebly had taken his place at the table reserved for the prosecutor. Peebly had the table covered with a widespread array of legal appearing papers, briefs, and a stack of issues of the Logan Station *Leader*, its news columns laden with accounts of the past week's events, its editorials condemning the evil state of affairs in Cimarron Bend.

Buck spotted the *Leader*'s publisher and editor, Conrad Quinn, in the courtroom, notebook open and ready to record this current event. His notes would add to his paper's coverage of the activities and urgings of the Ministerial Alliance, the Civic Betterment League, the appointment of Hynote, Hynote's killing, the advent of the Ku Klux Klan, its parade, the disastrous night raid on Cimarron Bend, all culminating here in Buck's arraignment on charges of graft, dereliction of duty, corruption in office—and whatever Caleb Hull, Jellico, and their cohorts thought they might make stick.

Buck felt that he was far from ready to defend himself, but he would do his best to try. He scanned the audience of heterogeneous Logan Station townsmen, and their wives. Buck helped Kaahti squeeze into a seat on the back row of benches lining the courtroom and walked up the aisle to enter the railing gate. He wondered how many of the townsmen present here were members of the Ku Klux Klan?

As Buck seated himself at the empty defense table, Bud Reed came in the courtroom's double doors and walked up the aisle, passing through the still-swinging railing gate to sit down beside Buck at the table. The bailiff came from the judge's chamber to announce, "Hear ye, hear ye. His Honor Judge Caleb Hull, of the County Court jurisdiction of Cimarron Territory. All stand."

Hull entered, and all stood.

The judge's gavel rapped and above the noise of people seating themselves Hull said, "We are here to arraign our

present sheriff, Mr. Buck Mather, on charges of malfea-
sance. Mr. Mather, are you represented by an attorney?"

"No, your honor," Buck replied, standing.

"Do you want an attorney?"

Buck said, "Yes, sir. But I haven't had time to hire one."

"Do you wish the court to appoint an attorney to represent you?"

Buck suspected that this was among the last things he
wanted the court to do. "No, sir. I'll try to represent myself
at this hearing."

"Very well," Hull nodded. "I'd like to call Deputy Bud
Reed to the witness chair."

County Attorney Marley Peebly arose quickly. "Oh—your
honor—this hearing is set as an arraignment, in which case it
is necessary only to prefer charges, and allow the defendant
to enter his plea. It is not customary to take testimony at an
arraignment—"

The vigor with which the Judge gaveled down the county
attorney was a sufficient indication of Hull's complete domi-
nance of that timid official.

"Thank you, counselor," Hull said blandly. "The charges
in question are not completely drawn. It is necessary for me
to ask Deputy Reed a few questions to complete the indictment."

Bud looked at Buck. Buck, with a nod of his head, motioned Bud toward the witness stand. The young deputy
was conspicuously nervous and uncertain. His face was
flushed as he got up and stepped up to seat himself in the
raised witness box. The bailiff swore him in.

Hull, his black robe accentuating the pink ruddiness of his
round head and sparse sandy hair, turned intently toward
the youthful deputy. Bud sat on the edge of the witness
chair, tensely unfolding and intertwining his fingers.

"Now, young sir." Caleb Hull's voice was unctuous, ingratiating.

A suspicion gradually formed in Buck, replacing his first

curiosity as to why Hull would want to solicit testimony from Bud.

County Attorney Peebly was standing. "Your honor, may I approach the bench?"

Hull glared at him impatiently. "For what purpose?"

Marley Peebly, thin to the point of skinniness, his face pimply and blotchy, was manifestly even more nervous than Bud. He stammered, "Why, to confer with your honor regarding what line of questioning I should undertake with this witness."

"Do not concern yourself, counselor," Hull said firmly. "I have a few questions prepared which I myself will ask prior to any further action in this proceeding."

That confirmed it for Buck. Caleb Hull, feeling himself on shaky ground after Seth Ray's statements before noon, was bound to have one purpose in mind. He hoped to trick young Bud into some admission that would make Buck look bad. Hull wanted this opportunity to make certain that public opinion would rest strongly on his side before defining his charges.

"I presume, Deputy Reed," Hull was saying, "that your duties required you to be frequently in Cimarron Bend."

"Well, no sir," Bud said. "Buck and I usually went over there together."

"Do you mean that you never went alone to Cimarron Bend?"

"Well, hardly ever," Bud answered.

"Hmmm. Why was that?"

"Well, Judge, you see Buck and I worked as a team."

"Could it be that Sheriff Mather did not trust you to go alone?" Hull asked harshly.

"Why no, sir. You see we had a way of working—" Bud hesitated. "Well, maybe he hadn't ought to have trusted me. You see, we had this Deputy Hynote—"

Hull cut in, "Just answer my questions, Deputy Reed. You say Sheriff Mather did not trust you."

"Did I say that? I thought I said he ought—"

"Young sir, I caution you again. You are to respond only to my questions."

"But—"

"Now you mentioned the special oilfield deputy Hyman Knote, alias Hynote. Did the sheriff travel to Cimarron Bend alone to—a—confer with said Knote in private?"

"Sure. How else was Buck going to—"

"Going to what, Deputy?"

"Well, to keep track of—"

"To keep track of the money Knote was collecting from various Cimarron Bend residents who were engaged in illegal activities?" Hull pressed in hard, leaning out between the twin, lighted gaslight globes on either side of his desk.

"We went to Cimarron Bend to stop that," Bud said stubbornly.

"For what reason did you propose to stop it?"

"Well, godamighty—"

"Could it have been because Sheriff Mather resented Deputy Hynote's intruding on his private province?"

"I don't understand what you mean."

"Now we reach a point I do not understand, Deputy Reed," Hull intoned sanctimoniously. "If your purpose was only to stop these illegal connections, why could you not simply have turned Hynote out of office, or even arrested him? Why was it necessary for Sheriff Mather to instruct you to kill him?"

"Buck didn't—"

Bud's protest was suddenly drowned and lost in a noisy disturbance that surged up in the area immediately behind the prosecution table. Buck looked down the row where, half concealed by the high oaken courtroom railing, the Reverend Mark Jellico was on his feet, muttering something about "the courage to carry out a fearful judgment." His voice rose stormily as he shouted, "I do understand, your honor. Reed is but a misled young man in the toils of this devilish Mather. The way of the wicked shall perish!"

His voice fell to muttering again—"the guilty must be scourged, even with fire"—his right hand thrust in the pocket of his baggy sack coat was jerking frantically, his face purpling in mounting frustration as the object at which he jerked resisted and he yelled, "This misled youth must be shown the fate of those who rise against the avenging angels. The wages of sin is death!"

Whatever was in the coat pocket at which Jellico so sweatily jerked, was caught. It tore the coat's fabric as the Reverend frantically managed to bring the ripping pocket above the courtroom railing, and Bud launched himself from the raised witness stand like a projectile.

As Bud came sliding across the defense table on his belly, he barely managed to interpose his body between Buck and Jellico as the explosion from the pocket of Jellico's awkwardly outstretched coat sent its missile hurtling toward the sheriff. Bud took the bullet in the meaty flesh of his shoulder. It drove through to strike Buck in the chest like a clenched fist but its killing force had been spent in its passage through Bud's meat.

Buck's hand, en route to his chest where the smashed and blunted bullet had thudded against his rib cage, actually caught the falling missile in his hand. He looked at the leaden slug curiously, surprised at the polished, bloodless look of it, even in the furrowed place where it must have been deflected by Bud's shoulder bone.

Bud had slid clear across the table and fallen into the narrow area between the defense table and the courtroom railing. Jellico, with the dumb-faced look of a stunned man, had finally managed to extricate the pistol from his pocket and stood examining, first the weapon itself, then the fabric of his coat pocket where the sharp claw of the brand new .32 caliber pistol's hammer had caught, tearing the cloth. In preventing him from drawing the gun, he had been forced to fire through the coat pocket itself, and now he began slapping at the powder burned hole the trajectory of the fired bullet had made. His sack-cloth suit was still smoldering.

Then, seeming to recall his mission here, he struggled to wedge his way through the pressing crowd massed around him, apparently for another try at shooting Buck. But Caleb Hull had at last had the presence of mind to come scooting down off the high bench. He reached the preacher. Hull grasped Jellico's arm, wrestled it aloft, and confiscated the pistol.

Kaahti had somehow made her way up through the crowd and was inside the rail, kneeling over Bud. Buck joined her. Bud was sitting up now, holding onto his bleeding shoulder.

"It took me too long to figure out what that son-of-a-bachelor was up to," Bud was complaining. "I ought to have been smart enough right at the first to see he was trying to get a gun out of his pocket. Then I could have got to him and stopped him from shooting."

"You poor dumb hero!" Buck Mather was sufficiently moved to feel moisture in the corners of his eyes. "The way it wound up, the only thing you could figure out to do was to try to get yourself killed and save my life."

Kaahti said urgently to Buck, "We'd better get him home."

"Yes," Buck said. He carefully examined the blood oozing shoulder wound and said, "Just a minute."

He stood up. "Judge Hull," Buck shouted for attention. "I'll be bringing charges against Jellico for carrying a weapon into a court of law, and for attempted murder."

Hull was ignoring him. Banging his gavel he called for order. As soon as he could be heard over the hubbub, Hull pronounced, "The court wishes to thank the Reverend Jellico for his diligence in bringing this confiscated revolver to produce in evidence. It is most unfortunate ,that it discharged accidentally while he was trying to offer it as an exhibit to the court. The hearing is postponed. Mr. Mather, you and your deputy are hereby warned not to leave this jurisdiction until the hearing has been rescheduled. Clear the court!"

The crowd gradually cleared out, with several of Jellico's parishioners working to escort their still-struggling preacher out of the courtroom. Among the stragglers, talking excitedly together as they took their time in leaving, Buck saw newspaper editor Conrad Quinn firmly implanted among the spectators' benches where he had been sitting since the opening of the hearing. His notebook rested on his knees. He was writing furiously.

Buck went out the railing gate and strode up to him. "Have you already figured out, Quinn," he asked, "how to make this look bad for Bud and me?"

Quinn looked up, his rimless eyeglasses balanced professorially on his aquiline nose. "Sir? I beg your pardon?"

"I wanted to know if you've already figured out how to make this look like some devilment that Bud and I engineered?" Buck repeated.

"Sir, the Logan Station *Leader* prints the news," the bespectacled Quinn said.

"News my tail bone!" Buck took no pains to prevent his anger from showing clearly. "You've slanted every news column you've written. Every one of them is against me and Bud, and your editorials are a hell of a sight worse!"

Quinn rose. "We just print the news," he insisted.

"How about all those editorials on what a den of iniquity Cimarron Bend is? How its sinful stains are spreading out to spoil the blessed purity of our wholesome society here in Logan Station?"

"Our editorials have done no more than to reflect the prevailing sentiment."

Buck studied Conrad Quinn. He was an ascetic man. with a long nose and thin features. Behind his spectacles his eyes were the pale blue of shallow water, but firmly fixed on

Buck. The man's hands were shaking. Buck felt temptation to use his fists on him, knowing he could easily beat this thin, lightweight man into insensibility. But a lifetime of restraint withheld him. What good would that do?

The publisher repeated, his voice unsteady with fear, but he said it anyway, "We print the news."

Kaahti had Bud on his feet and they were proceeding toward the courtroom exit. Buck looked up at the bench. Judge Hull had retreated into his chambers. The courtroom was almost empty. With a final baleful and threatening glance at the publisher, Buck followed Kaahti and Bud.

Doc Bell had intercepted Bud and Kaahti in the corridor. "I had a feeling some fireworks might erupt at this hearing," he was commenting. "Anyway, with everybody in town up here there wasn't much of any place else for me to go. Let's take him over to The Owl Drug Store."

At the drug store, with Bud flaked out on Asa Ray's cot behind the pharmacy counter, Bell applied his antiseptics and bandages.

"It's a good clean wound," he said. "Small caliber bullet. It appears to have gone almost straight through." Doc grinned at Bud, "You'll have an excuse to lay around about as long as you did when you tried to wrestle that lion." He turned serious then, "It was a mighty brave thing you did, son."

Bud looked at the sheriff, clearly yearning for Buck's approval. "Maybeso I done it right," he said. "Just this once."

Buck, embarrassed at feeling a little too choked up for normal conversation, nodded his head.

Bud said ruefully, "I thought I just might be making a fool of myself again, jumping out across the table like that, but when I saw the hole tear in Jellico's coat pocket, and that little piece of the hammer come sticking through—"

Buck reached in his own pocket and pulled out the blunted and scored .32-caliber slug that had hit him in the chest, then fallen into his hand. "If you hadn't. jumped out there," he said, "this little jewel would have wound up in my ticker instead of in my pants pocket. Here, Bud. You earned it."

Buck gave the bullet to Bud, and went to get the Ford.

XI

Buck drove home, with Bud protesting all the way that he was too danged much trouble for Kaahti to fool with. In the house, while Kaahti fussed over Bud, making him comfortable in the spare bedroom, Buck sat down in the rocking chair at the foot of the bed to scan the day's newspaper.

Having come out prior to the hearing, there was nothing in it about the arraignment other than the fact that it was scheduled to be held. It was the publisher's editorial that Buck read aloud to Bud and Kaahti, and he found himself wishing that he had read it before going to the hearing and so roughly accosting Conrad Quinn.

Quinn's comments were ambivalent, but they lacked the fire of some of his earlier editorial pronouncements. Buck sensed that, while Quinn feared to come out in open opposition to the Ku Klux Klan, that the editor was a good deal less than enthusiastic about vigilante law. Quinn's tempered sentences sounded almost like Seth Ray's comments earlier that morning.

The editorial ended, "Rather than prejudging Sheriff Buck Mather, perhaps we all should wait until the due process of the courts has been completed. In the American system of justice, the accused is considered innocent until proven guilty."

But as Buck turned on through the pages of the paper he found a full-page paid advertisement for the Ku Klux Klan. The ad was headed:

KU KLUX KLAN WARNING

FIRST, LAST, AND ONLY WARNING TO:

GAMBLERS, BOOTLEGGERS, HIJACKERS, GUNMEN, PROSTITUTES, LAWBREAKERS OF EVERY SORT,

WE ARE SWORN TO PRESERVE THE SANCTITY OF HOMES: THE VIRTUE OF WIVES, MOTHERS, AND DAUGHTERS.

WE ARE 100 PER CENT AMERICAN, READY TO MAKE ANY SACRIFICE FOR OUR BELOVED COUNTRY.

WE DEMAND THAT THE STAIN OF SHAME BE FOREVER WIPED FROM THE GOOD NAME OF THIS COUNTY.

NO LAW ABIDING CITIZEN NEED FEAR OUR COMING, BUT AT OUR APPROACH HE WHO DEFIES THE LAW AND COMMON DECENCY WOULD DO WELL TO CHANGE HIS COURSE.

LAW BREAKERS: YOU CANNOT ESCAPE US. WE KNOW WHO YOU ARE. WHAT YOU ARE. WHERE YOU ARE.

THE UNSEEN EYE IS UPON YOU ALWAYS. BY DAY AND BY NIGHT. YOUR WHISPERING IS AS A LOUD VOICE TO US.

WE MEAN BUSINESS.

CHANGE YOUR WAYS THIS HOUR LEST YOU BE STRICKEN AS WITH A LIGHTNING BOLT FROM A CLEAR SKY.

THE GOOD WILL WELCOME US: THE EVIL WILL MEET A SWIFT, STERN RETRIBUTION.

WE HAVE GIVEN FAIR WARNING.   BEWARE!

THE KNIGHTS OF THE KU KLUX KLAN

The bluntly threatening tone, the ominous wording of the advertisement, made it difficult for Buck to judge the publisher's motives. A newspaper has the right to refuse any advertising it does not wish to carry. Perhaps publisher Quinn's greed for the sizable sum the Ku Klux Klan paid him for that full page of space had helped Quinn overcome his possible personal objections to the Klan as an instrument of enforcing law and order. Perhaps whoever had brought the ad into the newspaper office had been so politically powerful and influential that Quinn hardly dared to refuse it.

Buck showed the Ku Klux Klan page neither to Bud nor to Kaahti. No use worrying them with such rabble rousing tripe. He turned on through the paper, and was even more surprised to find in the sacrosanct pages of the Logan Station *Leader*, a quarter-page ad for the Ruby Pickard Show.

Buck recalled seeing the lobby posters at the Folly Theatre the night he had taken Hynote to Cimarron Bend, ballyhooing this return engagement of Ruby and her girly show troupe. Buck folded the paper slowly. With both the Ku Klux page and the Ruby Pickard Show ad in the same issue, it looked to Buck like publisher Quinn's affection for the advertising dollars produced was obvious. The two ads were more expressive of the publisher's greed than they were of any personal principles or editorial policy Quinn might be trying to pursue.

"Bud," Buck said, "would you feel like stayin' here by yourself for a while tonight?"

Bud looked at him with astonishment, and grinned, "You think I need somebody to hold my hand, Buck?"

Buck scrutinized his robust young deputy. "I guess you're old enough to stay by yourself. I think you wouldn't mind havin' somebody hold your hand if it was the right somebody. But the fact is, the way I've been pilin' up the worries on Kaahti lately, I thought maybe it might make a nice change if I took her to the show tonight."

"Down to the Odeon?"

"No, the Ruby Pickard Show is playin' a' return at the Folly over in Cimarron Bend tonight. I thought maybe she might enjoy that."

Bud smiled widely again, "But not as much as you would, I expect."

"It's up to Kaahti," Buck shrugged.

She was smiling eagerly. She had been fussing with Bud's pillows, smoothing the counterpane, making Bud comfortable. Now she confirmed her desire for the trip to Cimarron Bend by saying quietly, "I'll go fix supper, then change my dress and get ready."

While this was going on, Buck made his own preparations for the journey—just in case. He went in his own bedroom and got the shotgun from where it stood behind the head of his bedstead. He broke it in half, stowed it in its case, and went out to the barn to stash the cased scatter-gun, with a box of shells, under the back seat of the Ford. Returning to the house, he stood thoughtfully for a moment, pondering the fact that, while under suspension, he was forbidden to carry firearms. Considering all the facts of the situation then he decided *the hell with it*, and returned to his and Kaahti's bedroom. From the chiffonier drawer he removed a short barreled .38-caliber Smith & Wesson revolver that under normal circumstances he would have considered little more than a toy, and stuck it in his pants hip pocket.

As they drove toward Cimarron Bend after supper, Kaahti did something she had frequently done before she and Buck had been married, but not recently. She scooted over in the seat to sit very close to Buck. During their courting days it had been a buggy seat she had scooted over in, but Buck found it no less pleasant in the bouncing front seat of the auto that Kaahti's Kiowa relatives called "smokey behind."

Somehow, it made the Ford's bounding over the Cimarron Bend road ruts a lot more pleasant with Kaahti's softness to bounce up against. Buck tried something downright reckless. He took his right hand off the steering wheel and put his arm around Kaahti. She snuggled even closer.

It suddenly occurred to Buck that as these exhaust-smelly

vehicles became more popular the roads would be full of them, kiting around the countryside with young males driving them with one arm and hugging a girl with the other. It wouldn't be safe for sensible two-handed drivers on the roads and streets.

He could not help but compare how much better it had been in the days of the horse and buggy. Then you could hang the reins over the dashboard and have both hands to court with.

"You've had more than your share lately," Buck said.

She looked, brown eyed and pretty, up at him. "My share of what?"

"Worries."

"*I* have?"

"That's what I said."

"How about you?"

"Well, it's different with me. I've been in this shoot-'em-up business all my life. It's got to where I don't give a damn."

"That would be the only thing that would worry me."

"What do you mean?"

"My husband, when you are paying attention to what you are doing, there is no better fighter alive than you. If you get to 'not giving a damn,' some of your enemies will kill you."

"That's not exactly what I meant," he protested.

She thought about this for a while, then nodded. "I see. Is it, then, that you perhaps mean that there's such a thing as being too careful and cautious?"

Buck was still pondering the compliment she had previously voiced. He grinned boyishly, baitingly. "You think I'm a pretty good man, huh?"

Kaahti did not rise to that bait. "Buck, I knew Gui-pago, Lone Wolf, Sahaumant, in their old age. As young men, all of them would have come to you first, if they were making up a war party."

He turned serious. "Well, that pleases me. I knew them too, of course. Still know Big Tree, Hunting Horse, and I remember both of them as young warriors. If I was riding into a hot place, where I wanted to be with someone I could depend on, I'd rather have one of those boys with me than anybody I've ever known."

"More than Bud?"

"Bud will do to ride the river with! He's a young stud who'd be welcome on anybody's war party!"

Kaahti agreed. "But Bud is still like too many young warriors. Too rash. Trying to count too many coups. Maybe he will settle down when he has to prove nothing more to himself."

"The day will come when Bud will be as solid as a rock stuck in the Cimarron River bottom," Buck nodded. "I kind of think maybe he's got there already. Going off half-cocked and killing Hynote sure sobered him down."

"That isn't what has steadied Bud Reed," she contradicted. "You have done that!"

"I've been trying," he admitted.

"You have been succeeding. For Bud it has been like learning any hard thing of many parts. One doesn't seem to be understanding it at all, until suddenly, all the parts seem to come together at once and you understand. It is a sudden thing."

Glancing away from the road, Buck stared down at the ruler straight part of her long black hair. "I'm going to have to quit bringing Bud home when he gets bloodied up. One of these days when he gets well he'll leave, and you'll go with him."

Kaahti leaned back in the seat, came at his ear with even white teeth, and bit him gently. "When that happens, you will be entitled to come after me and cut my nose off!"

Buck paid a little less attention to the road and leaned to kiss her straight Indian-Spanish nose. "That," he said, "would be a worse massacre than the one at the Tonkawa Hills."

The car rattled out onto the planks of the rickety Cimarron River Bridge and Buck fought to control it. The Ford barely missed charging among a ten span hitch of fractious mules they were meeting and the angry teamster yelled something at Buck about getting that rattle trap off the road and taking that gal to bed and Buck was glad he could not make out in detail all that the teamster had yelled.

They ran on past the team of frightened mules, and Buck dutifully began trying to pay more careful attention to his driving. It was hard to do with the fetching Kaahti sitting so temptingly beside him. Buck reflected on the happiness of his marriage and could only be glad that he had stayed single so long.

There had never been any struggle to decide who was boss in the years of their marriage. He deferred to her wishes, as she did to his. Discussion produced decisions, mutually arrived at. Not that the waters had always been smooth, they had been through plenty of rough water. But somehow both of them had always had the willingness to trim sail, to try the other tack, and their craft weathered the rough water as well as the long swells and the troughs.

As they neared Cimarron Bend they passed the burned out remains of Arles' Casino, a litter of black ashes crisscrossed by a few charred timbers lying awry across the remains of the native rock foundation on which Barney Arles' fancy gambling house had been built.

In Cimarron Bend, the saloon front of The Same Old Ikey's was a jumble of shattered glass and broken boards. Inside its dim interior Buck could see the wrecked bar, the litter of broken bottles. He wondered how much of Ikey's stock of whiskey those broken bottles represented, and how much of it had been carried off intact to oil the gullets of Ku Klux Klan members—strictly for medicinal purposes, of course.

Buck wondered where Ikey Price was now. Tar and feathers is a painful punishment, but Ikey had a knack for survival, as did Barney Arles and similar members of the breed of rascals who followed the oilrush boomtowns and made their living by their wits. They would set out to find a new oilrush, and open up in its boomtown. Other card sharks and bootleggers would flow in here to fill the vacuum Barney and Ikey Price had left.

There is no way to keep boomers from a certain amount of gambling and boozing, Buck knew. Barney and Ikey had been right about that. Buck had to pull in to park the Ford a goodly distance from the Folly Theatre. Evidently, from the number of men milling around town, Ruby was going to have as full a house as ever.

As they turned the corner to approach the Folly Theatre ticket window, a small clot of loafing men, across the street, drew Buck's attention momentarily. There were faces in the group that seemed familiar, young bucks he felt sure he had seen around the streets of Logan Station.

It occurred to him that there was no reason why he and Kaahti should be the only Logan Station residents sufficiently attracted by the renowned Ruby Pickard Show to travel to Cimarron Bend to see it, but he felt a passing curiosity as to why the young bucks across the street were not standing in line at the ticket window instead of wasting their time on the other side of the street. Maybe they were broke.

The admission price was stiff; a buck and a half a seat! Buck asked the girl in the glassed-in cage, "Any seats left?"

"A few," the gum-chewing cashier replied primly. "They'll be pretty close to the back."

She was right. Buck was able to see exactly three empty seats in the entire theater. They were all in the very back row, and widely scattered. It took him a while to arrange with five men to move down one seat so he and Kaahti could sit together near the middle of the row. It was a noisy crowd, and as Buck had worked his subtle persuasion on the roughnecks and roustabouts roosting in the back row, he thought again, one of many hundreds of times in his life, of what a considerable advantage it was to be six feet six inches tall, broad of shoulder, narrow of hips, and to have a friendly face and a likable grin to go along with the physical size.

As they settled into their seats it occurred to Buck to note that Kaahti was one of perhaps no more than five or six women in the entire theater. All the rest of the seats were occupied by men. This, at first, seemed normal enough to Buck. After all, the population of Cimarron Bend was nearly 100 per cent male, made up of men who either had no families or were unwilling to bring them to Cimarron Bend because there was still not a single school or church in the entire community.

But the crowded audience got more and more boisterous as curtain time approached, then passed by a couple minutes. Some of the rough remarks yelled across the theater by impatient men made Buck begin to wonder if he hadn't ought to have had better sense than to bring Kaahti to this place.

Three more minutes passed and as the jammed audience's impatience began to be expressed by rhythmic handclapping and stamping feet, a burly male candy butcher came striding down the center aisle. Harnessed to his bulging middle was a tray laden with phonograph records (of Ruby Pickard's singing Buck supposed), boxed candy and cigars, picture postcards, and books. The candy butcher did not go up on stage but paused among the clutter of musicians' empty chairs in front of the stage. He turned to face the audience.

"Ladies and gents." His voice was loud, nasal, and penetrating. "The most beautiful girls in the world are going to fill this stage in two minutes, so I'd better get in my two-bits' worth first."

Hoots and catcalls.

"Now you may be impatient, but I have a little item here that you'll get down on your knees and thank me for telling you about once you've seen it. It's the brand new official program of the Ruby Pickard Show, containing a beautiful individual picture of every gorgeous girl you'll see here before your very eyes tonight and, in every case, I guarantee you she ain't wearing enough to hamper your imagination ary bit in visualizing how she'd look if you was to take it all off."

To Buck, this sounded notoriously like the pitchman's spiel preceding a Kansas City riverfront burlesque show, and reinforced previous doubts. He had made a grievous error in bringing Kaahti here.

"Now that ain't all, gents. In addition to the full-page photos of the beautiful girls and hilarious comedians who'll have you laughing yourselves right out of your seats here in a few minutes—"

"You said two minutes ten minutes ago!" somebody yelled.

The pitchman winked at his heckler and rolled nasally on, "—you'll find a collection of the spiciest jokes you ever read. There's one about a college boy who goes into a cafe, see, and he thinks he's going to play a joke on the waitress so he acts like he's deaf and dumb. He's a big good lookin' guy, like all you boys are—"

A ripe razzberry issued from a blousy overweight woman a few seats in front of Buck and Kaahti.

"—anyway this handsome college boy points to his ears and his mouth, shakes his head, and makes all kinds of signs that he can't hear or talk, so the waitress brings him a pad and pencil and he writes out his order on it. The waitress reads it and, folks, what she yells back at the cook—thinkin' this fellow is deaf, see, and can't hear what she says—will have you laughin' your head off.

"There's another one about a traveling salesman who gets

stranded overnight at a farmhouse away out in the country and asks the farmer if he can stay all night. The farmer says, 'Wal, all right, mister. But you'll have to sleep with the baby.' Now just wait till you read about that 'baby,' and read what happened and I'll guarantee you'll more than snicker. You'll be whooping it up and telling that story to all your friends from now on! Now I hear the orchestra tuning up their fiddles and horns backstage, so I know they're ready to get the show goin', so I'll mention just one more thing, and that's these picture postcards I've got.

"They are the original 'French Nights' series, and once you see one of them you won't be without the whole set. These girls are posed in the altogether. In the nude. Stark naked. Not wearing a stitch. And believe me these French girls are mighty well endowed and sure know how to show it off."

The musicians began drifting out, finding their chairs, sorting and rearranging music. The pitchman finished off his spiel.

"Now while the or-késtra is getting ready to go and playing the overture I'll be passing among you to give you your one and only chance during the entire show to purchase these sexy items I've been telling you about. So don't pass up this single chance you'll have to own these hot items. You'll be cussing yourself from now on if you don't. They're sensational!"

The conductor of the orchestra came out of the wings, trotting down the stairs at center stage to a burst of applause, along with considerable hooting and yelling. He rapped his baton and the musicians launched into a lively medley of popular tunes beginning with "Ida, Sweet as Apple Cider."

Attendants began moving down the outer aisles, dimming the gaslight globes along the walls, giving the pitchman adequate time to work his way up and down the aisles, selling his wares almost as fast as he could get them out of his tray.

The orchestra drifted into "Meet me in St. Louie, Louie, meet me at the fair" as the pitchman worked back through the middle and toward the rear of the house. The light attendants had reached the stage apron and now started slowly back down the outer aisles, this time turning out each lamp completely.

This left the stage drop curtain brightly illuminated from overhead and from the gas footlight trough at the front edge of the stage. The dropped curtain displayed a garish painting of an idyllic landscape, a stream running off into infinity from its source among blue, snow-capped mountains forested with pines, and in the foreground bright yellow aspen growth.

It was surrounded by brightly lettered ads for stores both in Cimarron Bend and Logan Station, and left Buck thinking about what a decrease the Logan Station merchants would notice in their businesses once this wild boomtown dried up, as it was bound to once the oil was played out. Among the ads lettered around the garish landscape on the stage curtains were three, one for Arles' Casino, one for The Same Old Ikey's, and another showing only a towering and luxuriant cedar tree bearing little resemblance to the one that had actually existed in front of Etta Redmond's place. The legend across it read The Green Tree, with no mention at all of what that emporium of female pulchritude had purveyed. The orchestra swung into "Shine On Harvest Moon" and the curtain rolled swiftly upward. The show was on.

XII

The "bevy of beauties" onstage—there were eight of them—were really good-looking girls, overdressed in feather boas, sequined skirts, and brief, gaudy slip-on jackets. As the music changed to the waltz beat of "In the Good Old Summertime," the garments they wore began to slip off in rhythm to their dance routine. Then the tempo picked up again, and they became a leggy chorus of synchronized high kicking legs and sequin shimmering bottoms exiting to the deafening cheers of the audience.

They were followed immediately by two comedians, a dignified straight man entering from stage right and a baggy pants Dutchman coming from stage left. The Dutchman's lopsided walk with one foot in the footlight trough, the other onstage, cued the straight man's opening line, "You're drunk."

The Dutchman quickly corrected his walk and came on with both feet onstage, saying, "Thank gott. I thought for a minute there I vas crippled." He approached the straight man to hiss in a stage whisper, "Mien gott en himmel, mien wife looks terrible tonight."

The straight man knocked him flat. "You scoundrel! You're talking about the woman I love!"

Dutchman: (prone on stage, loudly asked the audience) "Did anybody here lose a roll of money with an elastic band around it?"

Straight man: (rushing forward) "I did!"

Dutchman: (getting up) "Vell, I found the elastic band!" He held up one of the girls' garters.

As the laughter swelled again, a lifted split in the stage cyclorama revealed Ruby Pickard, posed and beautifully gowned. A thunder of applause greeted her, establishing that the "Sweetheart of the Oilrush" line printed on her advertising posters was no self-conferred title. She came strolling toward the footlights and at the first slackening of the applause the straight man declared behind his half-raised hand, to the Dutchman, "Look at her. She's so young and pretty! I'm afraid one of these oilfield rascals might try to take advantage of her. Perhaps we should teach her what's right and what's wrong."

Dutchman: "Ve certainly should. You teach her vat's right!"

The comedians exited, the orchestra softened, and Ruby sang "Meet Me Tonight in Dreamland," her honey-husky voice having just the right balance of sweetness and sexiness to make every man in the crowd feel her words were directed only to him. The music bridged into the solid rhythm of "Bill Bailey Won't You Please Come Home," of which Ruby did two choruses, and left her audience literally howling for more.

Buck lost his regrets about bringing Kaahti. She was obviously enjoying it all as much as he was. The show rolled on toward intermission, through more music, a tumbling act, a knife thrower with Ruby as his target, openly adding to the audience's appreciation of her courage as she stood up there before the hard-flung flashing knives that thunked into the target board surrounding her.

She was very briefly dressed for the knife-throwing act and remained so for her jazzy rendition of "Alexander's Ragtime Band," which followed. Buck could not but marvel at how her dancing act between verses avoided the crude bumps and grinds familiar in burlesque, and at the same time excited the audience twice as much.

Ruby finished her song, took repeated bows, and the

straight man rejoined her in center stage. He came on rubbing his face curiously.

He asked, "Is my face dirty, or is it my imagination?"

Ruby replied, "Your face is clean. I don't know about your imagination."

"Let's get married," he suggested eagerly.

Ruby looked at him sweetly. "Marriage is too much work. You wash the dishes—make the beds, and then a couple weeks later you have it all to do over again."

Straight man: (referring to the slender g-string she was wearing) "How do you keep that during the winter?"

Ruby: "I wrap it around a moth ball."

Straight man: (confidingly) "Did anyone ever tell you that you are fascinatingly, divinely beautiful?"

Ruby: (coyly, blinking her lashes at him) "No."

Straight man: "Then where did you get the idea?"

Both exited to lively music as the chorus of eight girls came dancing on stage for the preintermission finale. Down front, in the darkness near the stage, as soon as the mid-show finale music began, Buck saw a group of seven men arise. They were making their way back through the theater's darkened aisle, and as they passed the end of the row in which Buck and Kaahti sat, Buck would almost have sworn that one of the men was Judge Caleb Hull.

Buck was at first amused that such a pious, righteous, and upstanding citizen would sneak over here to see the show. His amusement then gave way to the serious thought that this was the same brand of righteousness that had motivated the upstanding citizen who had patronized Etta Redmond's house, then later chosen to kill her to prevent any faint chance that word of his clandestine life might get back to his wife in Logan Station. The thought generated an even more serious, unnamed dread that began to grow in Buck and he turned to Kaahti to ask:

"How do you like the show?"

She giggled like a schoolgirl. "It's a little bit naughty"—

her brown eyes lifted to his face, seriously—"but I'm enjoying it. It's nice."

The candy butcher had come down the center aisle again
and taken his place before the orchestra rail.

"Friends," he yelled nasally, "I thank you for the kind
words you've said to me about the little items offered you
before the show began, and I've got two more. Now that
you've heard the little lady, the star of this show, Miss Ruby
Pickard, sing, I know you're going to want to take that
lovely little lady home with you. Now I can't offer her to
you in person [catcalls], but I do have here this fine gramophone record of her singing her most popular songs. I'm
going to make it available to you at an economy offer. And
right now, as a refreshment during this short intermission,
I've got a few boxes of Ruby Pickard chocolates to assuage
your appetite, or as a presentation to the lovely lady of your
choice.

"These boxes of candy are yours for the incredibly low
price of two-bits each, and what's more, each and every box
contains a valuable prize. Now you'll find such things as ladies' hosiery, watches, a diamond ring, all sterling prizes of
great value in these boxes. I hear the musicians about to
come out again so we'll have just a few minutes for you to
purchase these gramophone records and your candy with its
prize before the show is under way again.

"Just hold up your hand wherever you are and one of my
assistants will approach you. There, already, I see a hand,
and a lucky purchaser. What did you find in your candy
box? A pocket watch! Hold it up where the audience can see
it. Thank you, sir. There's another purchaser over there—"

Buck noticed that, strangely, it took the orchestra longer
to tune up for the second half than it had for the first. The
candy selling went on for fifteen or twenty minutes, accompanied by the discordant background of tuning fiddles and
tootling horns, while the candy butcher continued his pitch,
selling records and candy, having the lucky prize winners

hold aloft their prizes, and while Buck saw several boxes of candy sold, he always seemed an instant too late to see the prize held aloft. The hand seemed always to have gone back down by the time he was able to look in the direction the pitchman had been pointing.

During the candy sale, Buck saw two more Logan Station men get up and leave the audience. This time he definitely recognized them. One was the proprietor of The Dixie Store, the other his assistant manager. The interminable candy sale finally ended, though during the overture to the second part of the show the pitchman and his assistant kept on selling Ruby Pickard phonograph records through the audience.

As the lights dimmed toward final darkness a stage attendant appeared in front of the curtain drop to display a poster:

A DRAMATIC PRESENTATION

of

COLONEL STARBOTTLE FOR THE PLAINTIFF

(slightly adapted)

by

That Eminent Author of the Western Mining Camps

BRET HARTE

The curtain drop lifted to reveal the interior of a law office with Colonel Starbottle (the Dutch comedian now made up as a southern colonel type lawyer) seated at a roll top desk. The ingenue (Ruby Pickard) entered to ask the colonel to represent her in a lawsuit for breach of promise.

Colonel Starbottle protested hotly, declaring that breach of promise suits were dirty things, intensely disliked by him. Their shameful need to read love letters aloud in court invited ridicule "frightfully embarrassing to a man of my dignity and decorum."

Ruby (a "maiden with a prayer," the program note said) was made up as a country lass, with one front tooth blacked out, which did nothing to conceal her prettiness. She assured the colonel there were no love letters nor "nothing like that" to embarrass him. The colonel inquired the name of the guilty party who was to be sued, and was informed that it was Deacon Hotchkiss, of the Gospel Holiness Church.

Colonel Starbottle was awed that the eminent Deacon Hotchkiss should be so accused. Buck kept watching for the return of the Logan Station men who had left the audience prior to, and during, intermission. The seven who had left in the dark, among whom Buck was still inclined to believe he had seen Judge Caleb Hull, did not return. Neither did The Dixie Store owner, nor his assistant manager. It seemed extremely odd to Buck that these men would sneak covertly over here to Cimarron Bend to see what they would have considered an illicit show, then leave in the middle of it.

Onstage, Colonel Starbottle was declaiming in amazement, "Deacon Hotchkiss? And he wrote you no love letters. Then how can you prove breach of promise? How did the Deacon press his courtship?"

Ruby hesitated, then leaned to whisper long in the colonel's ear, while the colonel exclaimed, "He did?" and later, "Oh, my!" Then finally, "Not that!"

Ruby nodded. "He did!"

The colonel was horrified! "I'll take your case!" he trumpeted.

The curtain fell with a bang and the jugglers took over in front of it, while the muted noise of scene changing took place behind the curtain. When it rolled up again it revealed a mock courtroom, altogether too reminiscent for Buck to fully enjoy, recollecting the recent business of his own arraignment.

Ruby's girls, in male dress, filled the jury box onstage, the black-robed chorine who played the part of the judge was far removed from Caleb Hull's straw-haired pomposity, and

the straight man comedian had become skinny Deacon
Hotchkiss of the Gospel Holiness Church.

While Colonel Starbottle declared the contemptibility of
a church deacon taking advantage of an innocent young
girl, of not redeeming his promise, Ruby nodded, looking
coy, innocent, and wronged. Deacon Hotchkiss grimaced
with haughty mien, portraying superinnocence.

During the dialogue, Buck added up his own thoughts.
The group of men he had seen standing across the street
when he and Kaahti had entered the theater, and later the
departures before and during intermission now had him
thoroughly alarmed.

Buck leaned to suggest to Kaahti, "I think we better
leave."

She looked up at him questioningly, then quickly returned
her attention to the stage. Obviously, she was so enjoying
the show that Buck didn't have the heart to insist. He settled back in his seat with the thought, *Maybe it'll be safe to
wait till the end of this act.*

One of Ruby's chorus girls, wearing a cutaway coat to
play the part of the defense attorney, had arisen to demand
that the prosecution present its evidence, of which, she
insisted, they had not a single shred—no love letters—no
nothing. The defense attorney demanded the right to cross-
examine the plaintiff.

Ruby took the stand.

"No," she testified, "he didn't write me no love letters.
But he'd set a-side me in the choir of a Sunday morning, and
underline words in the hymn book—words like *love,* and
dear, precious, sweet, and *blessed.* One Sunday morning he
opened the prayer book to the marriage ceremony and un-
derlined whole sentences in it—the promises the groom
makes to the bride."

The defense attorney protested, "But he gave you no
gifts?"

Ruby: "Oh, yes. One morning when he passed the collection plate, he passed me one of them valentine peppermint hearts that says 'I love you.'"

Defense Attorney: "Would you produce it here in evidence. Please show it to the court."

Ruby: "I cain't. I et it."

Defense Attorney: "Still he never asked you to meet him anywhere, after church?"

Ruby: "He used to go, slinky, past our house at night after church and call 'kerrow' like a bird, you know, and I'd answer 'kerree' out the window, like its mate."

Defense Attorney: "But you never did actually go out to meet him."

Ruby: "Onct we went on a church picnic. He tolled me off out in the woods a ways."

Defense Attorney: "What did he do?"

Ruby: "He read me out of the Bible."

Defense Attorney: "From the holy scriptures?"

Ruby: "Yes."

Defense Attorney: "How utterly harmless! How inspiring. That Deacon Hotchkiss would take this lovely girl into the woods to teach her a lesson from the holy Bible. What did he read to you, my dear?"

Ruby borrowed the Bible the bailiff had used to swear her in. "It's over here in the Song of Solomon," she said, finding her place and beginning to quote, "'Let him kiss me with the kisses of his mouth—thy lips are like a thread of scarlet—thou hast ravished my heart—thy navel is like a round goblet—thy two breasts are like two young roes—'"

Deacon Hotchkiss jumped up from his place at the defense table, and ran to Ruby's lawyer, Colonel Starbottle. Pulling a huge roll of money from his pocket, the Deacon shouted, "I throw myself on the mercy of the court!"

He began counting bills off the roll of stage money, throwing them on the plaintiff's table; and the robed members of the Logan Station Ku Klux Klan came marching silently down both outside aisles and the center aisle of the theater.

XIII

Buck rose half out of his seat. He reached for Kaahti's arm, watching the Ku Klux Klan with their peaked white hoods file down the aisles. He realized then that it was too late, and sunk back down in his seat. The Grand Dragon, or whatever he called himself, marched up the steps to the center of the stage and turned to face the audience.

Flinging his arms out dramatically, his white-robed sleeves hanging down like broad white pennants of purity, he announced, "The foul, vile, filthiness of this performance is ended. The Knights of the Ku Klux Klan will permit no more of its obscene lewdness. We have heard the Holy Book defiled! Leave quietly and go in peace and you will not be harmed. If you refuse, we are armed and will take action against you!" He turned to face the wings. "Lower the curtain!"

As the curtain rolled down behind him, the audience's grumbling increased angrily, but the solid lines of Ku Klux, each armed with a visible pistol, rifle, or shotgun, had a remarkably sedative effect. It stunted the growth of excitability and anger as men slowly began filing out. Buck took Kaahti's arm again and they rose to join the crowd.

For Kaahti's sake, Buck slumped, almost stooping as he walked, seeking concealment in the anonymity of the crowd, and apparently succeeding. A knot of men had already gathered around the ticket window, yelling for the refund of their money, but the cashier's booth was empty. Buck escorted Kaahti on past it and around the corner.

They made it to the Ford. Wasting no time, Buck set the

throttle and the spark, and cranked it. As they pulled out
into the street, Kaahti was looking off across the flat at the
darkened old Turkey Track ranch house, which had been
Etta Redmond's brothel.

"I thought," she said, "that such places were busiest late
at night."

Buck said, "I'm sure the Ku Klux wrecked the inside of it,
just like they did The Same Old Ikey's. I noticed some windows were busted out on our way to the show. They killed
Etta—accidentally—and ran off all of her girls. I anticipate
that the Ku Klux ad in the paper will scare off any street-
walkers who might be tempted to try their luck here for
a while."

"What ad?"

He told her about it.

"Why didn't you want to show it to me?"

"Well, I didn't want to worry you. I ought to have done a
little more worrying myself. We're in a fix. It's likely that
some of that Ku Klux bunch saw us in the audience. If we
try to take the main road to Logan Station it's more than
likely we'll be caught up with—or waylaid."

Buck's thoughts were moving fast as he considered this.
Now he knew, well enough, what J. B. Wells had meant
with his whispered, covert, *Red Jaggers' pasture. Midnight
tonight.*

"I guess that maybe Etta Redmond was a bad woman,"
Kaahti was saying, "and maybe she deserved to be
punished. But no more than the men who bought her favors.
And she certainly did not deserve to die."

Buck, searching his mind for a way out of this, tried to
sound conversational with his comment, "That's pretty
much the way I feel about it." In his thoughts, he was mentally probing down an old cattle trail that had once made its
meandering way down from the cattle loading pens at the
Santa Fe Depot in Logan Station to the Turkey Track ranch
headquarters here in Cimarron Bend. It was no road, but

the countless cattle driven over it from the Turkey Track pastures to those railroad loading pens had left a wide trace. It had been in use up to only a couple years ago. Buck wondered if the Ford could negotiate that old trail, and so avoid the main road.

With certainty then, knowing that he had no other choice, he suggested, "Kaahti, I reckon we're going to have to make a stop on the way home." He told her about the secretive message J. B. Wells had delivered at the foot of lawyer Wooley's stairway.

"The Ku Klux will be going from here to that meeting at Red Jaggers' place," Buck told her. "I don't see any way I can avoid at least trying to find out what they are up to."

"Where is this Red Jaggers' house?" she asked.

They had turned off the rutted Cimarron Bend street. Buck was heading the Ford out across open country, as best he could remember, in the direction of the now long unused cattle trail. He could feel the tension in Kaahti, and he felt an equal surge of pride that she expressed none of it, even withholding any expression of doubt in him, or dread or fear of what might be ahead.

"They won't be meeting at Jaggers' house," Buck said. "He has a couple sections of upland pasture between the main road and the Summit View Cemetery just this side of Logan Station. They'll be in there in one of his pastures somewhere. They may be hard to find, but I've got to try."

She thought about this for a while. "If you are able to find out anything, what could you do?"

"It's hard to say," he admitted. "But as sure as the sun rises in the east, until somebody figures out a way to stop this Ku Klux outfit things are going to keep on getting worse. Maybeso the first fellows who crawl under those sheets have high ideals and lofty motives. But it don't take long for the other breed to find out this is a way to get even with their enemies, and do it from behind a mask. Then the sure enough owlhoots join up, and the looting, the burning, and the punishing, the 'accidental' killing just goes on and on."

"Where are we now?" she asked.

"This old time Turkey Track cattle trail wanders off across country and winds up at the Santa Fe depot loading pens in Logan Station."

"Do you think we can drive over it?" Kaahti asked doubtfully.

"We are sure trying," he said. The Ford was lurching violently over rough country, one of its wheels occasionally falling into soft ground left by the burrows of a coyote's den, or an abandoned prairie-dog village. The couple years' growth of chaparral since the trail had been used scraped the Ford's sides noisily.

"How will we get across the Cimarron River?" she asked.

"There's a low water ford where they used to drive the cattle across. The soldiers stationed at Camp Russell used to use it back in the eighties. They called it Five Mile Crossing—"

"You mean you're going to try to ford the river with this car?" Kaahti was incredulous. "What if there's quicksand?"

"We'll get stuck," he grinned at her in the dark.

She could not see his grin. "Will this car run in the water?"

"If the water doesn't get up over the exhaust pipe."

"My grandfather lost a horse in Cimarron quicksand," Kaahti said.

"The Rock Island Railroad lost a whole train in it when their trestle collapsed over by Kingfisher."

Kaahti moved up close to him again. "Well, my husband—"

"I'll be careful, Aadlemah," he promised, using a Kiowa pet name for her that he had not used for years. "This old trail intersects the section line road that travels right down the middle of Jaggers' twelve hundred and eighty acres. If I can just get up close enough to that meeting to hear what they're planning to do next, I can go to the capital and lay it before the Territorial Peace Officers' Association. Maybe I can get some help there."

They drove through the cricket-singing lanes of the night, watching the timber's myriad insect population swarming in toward the yellow cones of their headlights' glow, listening to the wind sough in the lonely high tops of the cottonwood and walnut trees which towered up into the darkness above the hardwood forest through which they crept.

As the country let down slowly into the Cimarron River Valley, the Ford made jumpy passage over washed out sandstone ledges. Buck steered with difficulty, wrenching the wheels to left, then right, trying to take some of the worst drop-offs at an angling course. Nearing the river the ground turned soft with dry, shifting sand, until they eased off the riverbank and out onto a long, wet, sandbar. It held firm as, slowly, they approached the dark, meandering current of the water.

The river current turned a dull and sullen red before their headlight glow. Buck eased the front wheels into the water. He could feel the wet sand giving away beneath them, and it seemed that Kaahti, beside him, almost stopped breathing.

The sluggish, muddy current took hold, tugging at the wheels. The Ford settled into the water, perhaps seven or eight inches deep here, flowing rapidly, but he could see before them none of the whorls or whirlpools that usually indicated a deep hole.

"Shame she can't swim like a horse," he said, attempting to sound relaxed and jocular. "I'd just give her her head."

Kaahti kept silent. She, as well as he, knew the treacherous nature of this sandy, salty river. The wheels crunched, without warning, on something beneath the surface. Undoubtedly a sunken tangle of brush, and the rear wheels spun futilely as the right front tire dropped more than hub deep. The front end swung with the current then, found footing, the rear wheels caught again, and the Ford lurched forward.

Now the whole car sunk bodily and Buck heard the exhaust pipe gurgle and mutter as it went beyond its depth. He gave her throttle, gently, tender footed with gentleness. . . . *Race her just a hair too much,* he thought, *and the back suction would inhale river water when his foot came off the throttle. She'd drown like a caught rat.*

"When she dies, Kaahti," he said, "get out, but don't panic. If we're in a deep hole, stay on the running board till the water, or the quicksand, gets to your armpits. I'll be coming out the same side you're on, to help you. Maybeso we can make it to dry ground."

"I am a strong swimmer," she said confidently. "But with all these clothes on . . ."

"That's what you're supposed to be doing while you're standing on the fender while she's going down. Take 'em off!"

Kaahti giggled, "We'll be a pair for somebody to find in the morning. A naked man and woman running around the woods like Adam and Eve—"

The Ford found bottom again and went a few feet farther, squeamishly, like someone suffering from loose bowels. The rear end fish-tailed sharply in the current, then suddenly found firm sand and resumed its steady creep toward the far bank. The current shoaled off and they were up on a sandbar again with only a narrow, and likely the deepest, channel of the river between them and the climb up out on the bank.

"What do you do if you get in quicksand?" Buck asked abruptly.

"Lie down," she replied. "Spread-eagle. Don't fight it. The harder you fight the faster you sink. Lay as flat and still as you can and scissor your arms and legs slow. Try to float it, and keep from getting in deep enough for it to suck at you."

"Just wanted to be sure you knew," he said. "Don't get scared."

Kaahti's giggle sounded very shaky. "And keep your clothes on," she finished.

Buck grunted. "They'll hold air and help you in quicksand," he agreed seriously, then the grim humor of the situation shoved irrepressibly at him. "Trying to undress in quicksand would be like trying to undress in a vat of molasses."

The Ford's front wheels hit the edge of that final stream of water in the channel. They dropped sickeningly, off a ledge of sand rock, then landed solidly. This last twenty or thirty feet of the stream's width was a channel almost eight inches deep, but running over a ledge of solid rock. It was like driving on paving during a heavy rainstorm. The Ford rolled across it slowly, but smoothly. The front wheels emerged on the far shore and the Ford began climbing the gradual rise of the riverbank.

"It's a wonder this old hoopy don't shake itself now like a wet dog," Buck breathed in relief. He looked in the rearview mirror. The rising moon shone, a clear reflection, across the three quarters of a mile wide river, its wet reddish-brown sandbars, and the split current, the two actual streams of running water, they had crossed.

"The Powder River, up in Wyoming"—Buck was talking as much to relieve his own strained nerves as anything— "they used to say it was a mile wide and a inch deep."

"That is not the way with the Cimarron." Kaahti seemed settled into her usual philosophical calm. "Usually it is not a mile wide, but I have seen it up to forty feet deep in flood times."

"An' damn near forty miles across when it was forty feet deep," Buck agreed.

They pulled up in a park which bordered on the river, an expanse of area cleared of timber but deep in grass. The Turkey Track cowhands had once used this as a holding pasture for trail herds, a place to rest the cattle and regroup after a hard river crossing. The Cimarron was often swimming deep when beef cattle had to be delivered to the Logan Station railhead after fall roundup.

Buck let the Ford's engine idle while he pulled out his bandanna and mopped his sweating face. He sat, relaxing for a moment, and said, "We've got about five miles to go to get to the cemetery road."

Getting up on his knees then, he reached across into the back seat and heaved up the rear seat cushion. He uncased and assembled the shotgun, inserted a buckshot loaded shell in the firing chamber of each barrel, thrust a handful of extra shells in his pocket, and laid the box of shells in the front seat between himself and Kaahti.

Just to be absolutely certain, he took the .38-caliber Smith & Wesson from his hip pocket, broke out the cylinder, checked it, and returned it to his pocket. Then he resettled himself under the steering wheel, and shoved the Ford's pedal into low gear. They ground out the next couple of miles through the high grass and chuck holes of the trail in silence, with Buck wondering if he had any chance at all of locating the Ku Klux in twelve hundred and eighty acres of pasture land, providing J. B. Wells had been right about their intention to meet there. How in the world had he ought to go about hunting them?

That turned out to be no problem at all. As they began climbing up out of the lowlands of the Cimarron Valley, Buck saw a faint red glow against the sky, ahead and off to the right. Almost instantly, he guessed what he was seeing. At the mile intersection before reaching the cemetery, he turned off the trail they had been following.

This road ran westward, at first skirting, then cutting through Red Jaggers' ranch land. The glow against the sky grew perceptibly brighter as the Ford ran toward it. A mile before reaching the main Logan Station road, the red glow was at its brightest, and just over the hill to their left. Here, also, was a gate in the three strand barbwire fence alongside which they had been driving. Buck stopped, got out, opened the gate, and drove through.

As he closed the gate after he had driven through, and returned to the car, Buck figured this would doubtless be a rough trail Jaggers had hacked out of the blackjacks so he could short-cut in here to feed his cattle in the winter. He was right. It angled up the hill, obstructed by stumps often so high he was afraid one of them would drag the bottom out of the car.

A couple of the stumps touched, each a grating threat to rasp at his nerves and make him grind his teeth with worry. Through all this Kaahti sat quietly, apparently composed, but Buck knew better. She was sharing every nerve-racking worry with him, but bearing it all with a composure more even than his.

The Ford continued its upland climb until they had crested a hilly knob tightly entangled with the solid blackjack forest of this cross-timbers country. Beyond the knob the red glow was flickering brightly. The narrow trace through which they had so slowly driven was barbwire fenced on both sides, so Buck got out, opened the tool box bolted to the car's left running board, and secured a pair of wire cutters.

He cut the fence. Turning off the trail then, he drove the Ford deep into the timber, wincing each time he heard the underbrush or a gnarled blackjack branch grind and scrape away the paint from the sides of this still almost new car of which he had been so proud. What with the Cimarron salt and sand, the brush, the coyote and prairie dog holes through which he had put that little Ford this night it would be ready to be thrown away with the tin cans and trash back of the house by the time he got it back to Logan Station.

Presently, feeling that the car was as well concealed as possible, he eased to a stop. He reached beyond Kaahti to grasp the double-barreled shotgun, and put it into her hands.

"Don't use it unless you have to," he warned her. "It will sure give away where you're at. But don't let them Ku Klux get close to you either. I'll be back as soon as I can."

XIV

Buck slid out over the dummy front seat door and set out through the trees as quietly as he could, considering that the timber floor was covered with years' accumulation of fallen, dry blackjack leaves. The moon, high and sufficiently bright to cast shadows, made the leaf covered earth a shadowy latticework from the interlaced tangle of branches and vines above him.

As he approached the timber's edge he could see that he had been right. Knowing that he and Kaahti had been the first to leave, and that there was no shorter route than the one they had taken, in spite of the rough going over the abandoned cattle trail and necessity of fording the river, Buck felt certain they had to be the first to arrive here from Cimarron Bend.

But sure enough, as he stood here where the timber rimmed the pasture, less than fifty yards from it, he could see it plainly. A huge, burning fiery cross. Squatting near it, smoking roll-your-own quirlies and talking, were four Ku Klux, all properly unidentifiable in the anonymity of their white robes and peaked white hood masks. A committee sent out from nearby Logan Station, Buck figured, to prepare the meeting grounds.

They had erected the huge cross of creosoted railroad ties, wrapped with gunny sacks soaked with kerosene, and set it afire. One of the committee of four got up at that moment, picked up the empty kerosene cans, three of them, and carried them off toward the section line road which ran along the west edge of Jaggers' pasture.

The retreating Ku Klux gave Buck a thought and, skirting along the edge of the timber, he followed him. Sure enough, tied to the barbwire fence along the road, were the horses two of the Klansmen had ridden out from town, along with the team and spring wagon that had brought the other pair. The burning cross was a beacon light of towering flames on which Klan members from miles around could home in. It would guide the posse of raiders who had closed down the Ruby Pickard Show in Cimarron Bend over here from the main road, just as it had guided Buck and Kaahti up from the Cimarron Valley lowlands.

The Klansman deposited his kerosene cans in the bed of the spring wagon and started the climb back uphill toward the burning cross. This was an area where Red Jaggers had cleared out a wide loop from the surrounding timber to form this perhaps ten to twelve acres of land. The pasture was widest where it bordered the section line road, narrowest where it circled back into the blackjacks toward Skeleton Creek.

The fiery cross was burning, roughly in the center of the native grama and buffalo grass pasture. As the Klansman who had left the kerosene cans in the wagon returned to the burning cross Buck straddled the barbwire fence and concealed himself in a clump of five-foot-high sumac brush beside the fence. He was hoping.

One of the horses neighed and his hopes rose. But the coming horse the neigh had signaled was not being ridden. It pulled a buggy, in which two robed Klansmen were riding. The buggy whoaed to a halt not ten yards from where Buck hid, and its occupants got out. As they crossed the fence Buck heard a ripping noise, and one of the Klansmen cursed briefly, complaining he had torn his pants on a barb.

Buck felt a considerable temptation to rise up and tell them that, in his opinion, anybody who joined the Klan had, figuratively speaking, tore his own britches. But he laid low, and was rewarded some ten minutes later. A lone Klansman came riding up, dismounted, tied his horse, and as he approached the fence Buck swarmed all over him from the rear.

Buck wrestled the Klansman to the ground, choking him with an iron grip around the man's jugular, Buck's other big hand over the Klansman's mouth and pinching his nose shut with thumb and forefinger. The downed Knight had been unable to utter a single sound and his struggles weakened and ceased as Buck suffocated him.

As soon as the man was still Buck eased up. He had no desire to kill him, and as the Klansman tried to regain consciousness, pumping air with tortured rasps into his starved lungs, Buck stripped off his mask, then used the Klansman's handkerchief and his own blue bandanna to gag him. Taking off the Klansman's robe then, Buck flipped open his jackknife. He cut a leather bridle rein from the man's horse, tied the Klansman's feet and pulled them roughly back and up to his wrists, leaving him helplessly bound.

Buck dragged the Ku Klux over into the sumac where he had been hiding, and donned the man's white robe and mask. Only then did he take time to take a close look at the Klansman's face and identify his victim. Buck knew him. He was a young, pimple-faced flunky who worked at the Cimarron Valley Creamery, next door to Talmadge's livery barn.

A flaccid muscled youth whose heaviest work was counting and candling eggs, he had been an easy victim. He stared up at Buck, not with anger, but with horrified and terror-stricken eyes.

"Take it easy, son," Buck told him. "Don't try to get loose, and don't make any fuss, or I'll have to raise a knot on your head. Just be quiet, and behave."

Buck settled down in the sumac to wait.

He studied the star filled sky above him and concluded that it was a little past eleven-thirty, probably fifteen or twenty minutes before midnight. Plenty of time for the contingent that had gone to Cimarron Bend to arrive here at the appointed hour, midnight. It struck him suddenly that tonight, June 27, was the night of the full moon. Maybe that had something to do with the craziness of the Knights of the Ku Klux Klan.

He looked up, and there it was. Eleven-thirtyish high, as full, round and bright as a William Jennings Bryan silver dollar. With the help of the fiery cross, it was lighting up the clearing in the pasture, and the surrounding timber, almost as bright as day. And then he heard them. The low-throated growl of an approaching convoy of motors.

It made sense. The Ku Klux who went to Cimarron Bend would have been able to command a sufficient number of motor vehicles to return together all in a bunch. He saw the reflection of their headlights then, bouncing up and down along the road, approaching from the cemetery road.

They turned right when they reached the Jaggers' section line and were coming toward him. He could make out a pair of T-Model Fords, an Overland, a Studebaker and, sure enough, Roy Stribling's Stanley Steamer. Roy Stribling was the owner of the Floradora Pool Hall. The Klan had opened the doors of righteousness pretty wide, Buck decided, in recruiting their members.

Last in the procession was the Kalb Dray and Storage Company's big flatbed truck. The truck bed was loaded with white-robed Klansmen. Assuming four or five Ku Klux Knights in each of the preceding autos, another ten or twelve in the truck bed, the total number of Klansmen approaching was nearly certain to exceed thirty, Buck figured.

The procession slowed, stopped, and began to shut their motors down. The motorized caravan completely blocked the single lane section line road. Ku Klux Knights began to climb out of the cars, one or another occasionally having trouble untangling the long white robe in which he was gowned, and to which he was obviously unaccustomed. Buck noted that several also had trouble with the peaked hoods pulled down over their heads, masking their faces.

They hung together at first, in clots of three or four, each
tending to stay in the group with which he had ridden from
Cimarron Bend. The mutter and murmur of their conversation was muffled, solemn, serious, portentous, sounding to
Buck as if they were vastly overimpressed with their own
importance. He made no effort to sort out individual phrases
of this pompous small talk, just being diligent about hunker-
ing down low in the sumac thicket in the hope he wouldn't
be spotted in the near floodlight effect of the bright moonlight.

As the bunch of Knights of the Ku Klux Klan spilled down
off the flat bed of the dray truck the whole crowd of them began to mix and mingle as they moved toward the fence, and
Buck simply stood up and joined them. He noted a hood or
so turn his way as he moved in among them, but if anyone
had noted his prior squatting position in the sumac thicket
they must have decided he was simply answering a call of
nature in doing so. At least no one questioned him.

The Ku Klux helped each other across the barbwire fence,
shoving sagging sections of it close to the earth with boots
or shoes so others could cross. He heard someone, probably
Red Jaggers himself, complaining of the treatment to the
fence and suggesting that somebody better show up tomorrow to help him restretch it and staple it to the posts.

By the time they were all across the fence the crowd of
Ku Klux was pretty well strung out across the pasture. Some
protocol must have been observed in the fence crossing for a
small group had more of less taken the lead in the procession, and one, rather large in his robes, seemed headed
directly for the fiery cross.

Buck's robe came only to his knees. The Ku Klux Knight
he had waylaid had been a good deal shorter than Buck so
he tried to mingle with the majority and be as unobtrusive
as possible. Most of the Knights' white robes literally swept
the pasture grass. All were closing in on the hotly burning
cross now and Buck glanced back down the slope to see that

two white robed and hooded figures still remained standing up on the bed of the truck, partially concealed by its low side boards.

Too busy moving and mingling and keeping a low profile to wonder why those two still remained in the truck, Buck watched the heavy-set "Grand Dragon" take what was apparently his official position in front of the fiery cross. He lifted up his arms much in the same way as when he had faced the audience from the stage of the Folly Theatre.

"Brother Knights of the Ku Klux Klan," he called for their attention sanctimoniously, sonorously, and Buck knew that voice but could not quite connect a face with it.

"Let us unite our hands," urged the singsong voice, "and all march in a circle around this blazing emblem of right in a spirit of brotherhood and klannishness."

There was an awkward joining of hands. A few Klansmen had no weapon in sight, but most carried either a rifle or a shotgun. Buck took a sort of half overlapping hold of his nearest neighbor's hand around the stock of a .30–.30 rifle the Klansman carried. The fellow on the other side of him was one of those with no weapon in sight, but Buck felt sure he would not have to feel around the pocket areas beneath the Klansman's robe long before he found a hogleg of some kind.

The Ku Klux began a jerky circling of the fiery cross. *Ring Around the Rosie*, Buck thought, his mind having trouble coming to grips with the puerile, childish silliness of it, in contrast to the danger loaded potential he knew this situation held. Someone on the far side of the circle began singing and, raggedly, other hoarse voices took it up until most were singing:

> *"Onward Ku Klux soldiers*
> *Marching as to war*
> *With the cross all blazing*
> *Going on before—"*

It was an out-of-tune cacophony. *Ludicrous,* Buck thought, *to watch grown men in white nightshirts and pointed caps, trying to hang onto each other's hands, singing a psalm tune like a bunch of reluctant Sunday-school boys.* But they were going at it determinedly, and loaded with enough visible armament to take on a Hessian regiment in a head to head gunfight.

His subconscious told him, too, that he knew the voice that had started up the song. He had never heard that voice sing before, but he felt sure that if he could hear that same voice talk he could put a name to it. The sorry singing went on, and the marching kept up,

> *"Forward into bat-tle*
> *See our banner go—"*

They had made a complete circle around the fiery cross, with Buck winding up a little beyond where he had started, still trying to hold hands with the men on each side, as the song ground down to its weary end.

> *"Onward Ku Klux Klansmen*
> *Marching as to war*
> *With our fiery emblem*
> *Going on before."*

The head man out in the middle lifted his arms again, in his now familiar dramatic gesture, and cried out:

"Brother Klibe, come forward and approach this sacrosanct station of exalted authority!"

Clibe, Clibe, Buck thought earnestly, *I don't know anybody in Logan Station named Clibe.* A fat Klansman detached himself from the circle to approach the head man.

"Exalted King of Knights," he said, "I wait your superior wisdom and exalted orders."

"Read the minutes of our last meeting."

He's the secretary, thought Buck, *and I've got to get my hands on that book of minutes he's reading from.*

When the droning reading of the minutes had ended the Exalted King of Knights summoned in a loud voice, "Brother Kloven, come forward."

The head man doesn't call himself the Grand Dragon, it got through to Buck, *he's called the King of Knights. There's a Kloven. Everything begins with a K—so Klibe, like Scribe.*

The King of Knights was saying, "Sir Kloven, do you stand ready to take instant charge of this meeting in case something happens to me?"

Buck was still trying to identify the King of Knight's voice as the Kloven replied, "I am ready, Exalted King of Knights."

Klaptrap! Buck thought, and grinned under his hooded mask at his own pun. The Klibe had moved to stand on the King of Knight's left; the Kloven, in long military strides, stepped to the King of Knight's right side. *He's the vice-president,* Buck decided.

The King of Knights howled out, "Is the Knighthawk within the sound of my voice?"

The shouted reply came from a clump of trees about halfway down the hill. *So they've posted a guard to keep an eye on us all,* Buck knew.

The King of Knights howled out his orders, "Let the Klaliff—" Buck had heard Caleb Hull's voice pronounce the word "bailiff" too many times to be mistaken. He knew who the King of Knights was. Having no idea how it might be with other Klaverns of the Ku Klux Klan, Buck had no doubt that Caleb Hull had made up this whole rigamarole in his own head, including the code names of its officers.

"Let the Klaliff bring forth the transgressors," Hull was shouting, "that they may be punished for their transgressions. Let the Klud bring the instruments of torture!"

Well, by all that's wicked, Buck thought, *they aren't making any bones about it.*

The corner of his eye caught movement at the foot of the hill. Turning his attention there, Buck could see that the two robed Klansmen who had remained in the truck that had brought up the rear of the procession from Cimarron Bend were busy. They were unloading two prisoners from the flat bed of the big dray and storage vehicle.

As the Klaliff and the Klud came herding the pair up the slope, the atmosphere among the encircled Klan members reached a peak of almost breathless silence. *A mob like this can hardly keep from turning bloodthirsty,* Buck thought. Even in the open pasture the smell of sweaty men, taut with sadistic waiting, permeated the still air.

Buck had smelled that odor before, among the mob that had surrounded the KC ranch cabin where Nick Ray and Nate Champion had been holed up, back in Johnson County. As the Klaliff and the Klud passed the clump of timber where the Knighthawk was hidden, Buck saw that the pair of prisoners they drove before them were a male and a female. He was startled then to note that the male prisoner was Wiley Lester. A moment of grudging admiration edged up through Buck as he mentally complimented the Ku Klux on being able to catch up with that slippery character.

His moment of admiration was instantly stifled by utter astonishment as he recognized the second prisoner. She was Ruby Pickard, the sweetheart of the oilfields. *These Ku Klux must be crazy,* Buck thought. *That showgirl is the ideal of the roughnecks and roustabouts in every oilrush boomtown in this territory. If this bunch hurts her, they will mighty quick change from being the pursuers to the pursued. A Knight of the Ku Klux Klan's life won't be worth a dime.* The cold certainty of this dominated Buck's thinking. *If the same thing happens to her as happened to Etta Redmond—*

The circle of Klansmen parted to admit the Klaliff, the Klud, Wiley Lester, and Ruby Pickard. The Klud, whoever he was, in his horny right hand carried a coiled up blacksnake whip. Buck's first astonishment at recognizing Ruby Pickard now gave way to an equal surprise in noting how young she was. Seen up close, without the stage make-up and the strange reflections of the Folly's gas footlights, it was clearly apparent to Buck that she could be no more than twenty or twenty-one years old.

It seemed incredible to Buck that a girl with so wide, and so wild, a reputation could be so very young. Her garish makeup on the stage had added some years to her appearance that she simply had not attained.

The Exalted King of Knights, his voice besotted with sadism, instructed, "Sir Knights, inflict the punishment on these transgressors!"

As the Klaliff and the Klud flung Wiley Lester to the ground, the Kloven and the Klibe stepped out to throw the girl down beside him. Lester's hands were tied behind him. So were Ruby Pickard's.

The Klud stepped back, adroitly uncoiled his blacksnake, letting it lay out across the prairie grass, then skillfully flung back his arm and delivered the first lash to Wiley Lester. The girl was trying to rise to her knees, her eyes bright with terrified horror.

Buck had to credit Wiley Lester then. The holdup man only grunted and squirmed with pain beneath the stinging bite of the blacksnake, but Ruby Pickard screamed piercingly, and one thought dominated Buck completely. *The girl is going to get it next.*

Never consciously willing himself to do so, Buck's hand whipped up the tail of the white robe he wore and he drew the .38. It was cocked as his hand came around, and the trigger already pulled, so that as his thumb released the hammer the .38 fired. The Klud's arm was flung back to lay the lash across Ruby's slight shoulders. Buck's bullet entered the Klansman's wrist just above the handle of the blacksnake whip, tearing open a bloody furrow from the man's wrist to his elbow.

The Klud spun toward the direction of the shot with a scream more piercing than Ruby Pickard's. He looked at the blood, spurting to stain the sleeve of his white Ku Klux robe and shrieked, "I may never be able to use my arm again!"

Buck backed slowly from his place in the circle, hand aloft, gun steadily pointed. "Stand fast, or you may never use your mouth again," he told the bleeding Klud.

Buck knew he was in trouble, sure enough trouble. It passed through his mind, a flash of strangeness, that he was in about the same position that Bud had been, in the lions' cage at the circus. All he could do now was bluff. Yet, perhaps more strangely, in the same instant, he recalled an old trick he had learned from Hynote, and had often practiced with that hard living, hard shooting individual during the long days of waiting between the incidents which involved actual shooting in the Johnson County War.

Buck pulled up the left side of his robe and reached in his pants pocket for one of the shotgun shells he had dropped in there after assembling the shotgun for Kaahti. He tossed it in the air, watching it rotate slowly in the reflected light of the fiery cross.

As the brass percussion cap of the buckshot loaded shell rotated down toward him then, Buck elevated the .38 and triggered it. He hit the percussion cap of the shotgun shell squarely, and the shell exploded in midair like a bursting of Fourth of July cannon cracker.

It was a dangerous trick—for the exploding shell sent flying buckshot off in every direction. But somehow Buck found himself unable to build up any concern as to whether any of the buckshot hit a Ku Klux Klan member.

Into the hollow quiet that followed the gunfire, Buck said succinctly, "I don't want to leave any doubt in anybody's mind that I can shoot straight. There are four shells left in this thirty-eight. If any of you jaybirds even give me a hard look, four of you are going to die."

The Exalted King of Knights corrected him, "Five! Mather, I know your voice and you must realize by this time that several of us here are sufficiently dedicated to your removal from office, by death if necessary, that no matter how many of us you get, someone among us will kill you."

Buck had no doubt of it. He was convinced that there was probably a higher percentage of fanatics among this bunch than he would be likely to find anywhere outside of a holy roller camp meeting. *What do I do next?* he thought. *It sure would be nice to see all their armament stacked up there in front of that fiery cross.*

Then he came at it from a different angle. *If I was lucky, and succeeded in making them unmask first . . . No,* he decided, *they'd kill me for sure then because I'd know who each one of them is.* The doubt that he could pull off either maneuver was far too serious.

However successful he might be in bluffing them into disarmament, it seemed a cinch that someone among them would manage to hold out at least a handgun with which to shoot him. Maybe his best bet was just to pick out the four he wanted to be sure went down and open the ball by killing them outright . . . that would be Hull, and the Klud, Buck decided, but of the other three Klan officers he would have to pick two . . . and Buck found his mind muddling around trying to decide whether they should be the Klibe and the Kloven, the Kloven and the Klaliff, or the Klibe and the Klaliff . . .

The rifle shot came from the clump of timber from which the Knighthawk had shouted, and Buck at first figured it was the Knighthawk shooting. Perhaps that mysterious functionary had finally decided the time had come to pick him off. But Buck felt the impact of no bullet. Instead, a shower of sparks flew from the fiery cross.

Immediately after the first rifle shot sent its shower of splinters out of the fiery cross, a second one sounded, from deep in the timber, and from the direction directly opposite the first shot. The briefest idea that the first shot might have been fired by Kaahti fled Buck's mind. She had no rifle. The second shot, from the opposite side of the circle of Ku Klux, had also 'orn a shower of sparks from the fiery cross.

XV

The two shots, coming from opposite directions, left Buck in confusion. The rifles spoke again, ripping twin showers of sparks from the Ku Klux' blazing emblem. Each of these shots came from the same general quadrants as the first pair, but each was a good thirty yards removed from its predecessor.

As the sporadic rifle fire from opposite sides of the Ku Klux circle continued, inspiration struck Buck Mather. Whoever was out there and shooting, and however many there were of them, the fiery cross was consistently their target. Each succeeding shot tore its own burst of sparkling fire from the burning burlap and creosoted wood of the cross.

The loud cracking echoes of each shot bounded and ricocheted through the surrounding timber until it began to sound as if Coxey's whole army was out there. The re-echoing noise and exploding sparks bursting from the target cross became an overawing exhibition. One of those shooters out there was banging away with a big Sharps buffalo gun.

Another rifle had a nasal whang reminiscent of Bud Reed's Winchester '73. When all the shooting stopped, suddenly, as if on cue, Buck followed through with his inspiration.

"All you mystic Knights of the Ku Klux Klan," he yelled, "listen." His voice loud, steady, and firm. "You know what the situation is. You are surrounded by the members of the Territorial Peace Officers' Association." Buck walked out into the center of the circle, taking a place a few feet in front of the bullet-splintered but still burning cross, standing there as comfortably as if he were in the center of his own living room at home.

"I had to wait to be sure that all the Association members were in place," Buck said flatly, "but if any one of you moves now this place is going to be remembered the same as that hill up on the Rosebud where the Sioux caught up with Custer's Seventh Cavalry."

"I want you to start moving up, slow and easy," he ordered. "Stay in line. Stack your weapons right here in front of the fiery cross."

The display of fireworks and target shooting had apparently been enough to move at least the timid to obedience. In parallel lines, they began shuffling up toward the flickering light cast out over the prairie grass by the burning remnants of the cross, and depositing their armament. Even the Kloven moved into the line, drawing a heavy horse pistol out from somewhere under his robe, and putting it on the growing pile.

"Wiley," Buck suggested to Lester, "you pick up one of them weapons and help me keep an eye on this situation. Miss Pickard, can you handle a firearm?"

The Exalted King of Knights, Caleb Hull, and the Klibe, stood without moving. The fat Klibe began jerking spasmodically, like a hand puppet, or an afflicted human about to have a seizure. Reaching between the pearl buttons that held together the front of his robe he jerked out his .32-caliber pistol, tearing the facing of his muslin robe with the frantic force of his haste.

Shouting "The Avenging Angel of the Lord will not be denied!" the Klibe ran toward Buck.

Shocked that he had failed to recognize Jellico before, Buck tried to cope with the sickening feeling of failure. He should have taken some precaution in dealing with him, and prevented this.

The preacher who had promoted himself to the permanent rank of Avenging Angel was coming headlong, running toward Buck between the parallel lines of Klansmen moving to lay down their firearms. Protected from sideline rifle fire by the lines of Ku Klux, Jellico seemed determined to get so close to Buck that he could not miss.

He was holding the pistol directly in front of his own fat body, and as the round hole in its barrel end came in focus and sharply distinct, Buck knew he was going to have to defend himself, and that he was going to have to shoot to kill.

The shotgun blast came from the timber, a considerable distance away, and behind the fiery cross. As its buckshot charge came sweeping across the pasture grass Buck's nemesis, the Reverend Mark Jellico, charging like the devil rather than any kind of angel, was caught full in the back.

Blown forward by the charge, he went sliding on his belly and face. Jellico wound up almost at Buck's feet. One of the stray buckshot hit Buck just below his hipbone, in the meaty part of his thigh. It stung meanly as it broke his skin but did not penetrate, and Buck knew it was better than a .32-caliber bullet between his eyes or the necessity to kill the preacher would have been.

That the shotgun blast was Kaahti's contribution Buck had not the slightest doubt. Thinking *son-of-a-gun, she always seems to be in the right place at the right time,* he stepped across the prostrate Jellico to pick up the preacher's .32. Buck then circled on around the fiery cross to retrieve the Klibe's book of Ku Klux records from where Jellico had dropped it. Buck thrust the book up under the white robe, locking it beneath his arm.

Turning then to face the Klan, Buck lifted off the hooded mask he had been wearing. In a voice good and loud he ordered the milling Ku Klux, "All right, gents. It's your turn. Let's see who you are."

A silence fell and the milling stopped. Buck yelled again, "Mind now! We don't want to have to start shooting them hoods off your heads!"

The rifleman in the woods who had been firing the big .50

buffalo gun took the hint. With a resounding blast he pulled off a shot and the heavy slug of the .50-caliber Sharps tore off the whole remaining top of the now splintered fiery cross.

Hooded masks began to come off.

"Pile them up here on top of the guns, boys," Buck ordered. "Hoods, robes, the whole works."

The act of being forced to unmask seemed to have a powerful effect on the Klansmen. Like shorn sheep, they shuffled back away from the burning cross, guttering now, as its flames burned themselves out.

Buck could hear embarrassed coughing and throat clearing here and there, and the guilty shuffling of feet in the prairie grass sounded like a multitude of small animals scuttling about.

In a night of surprises, he could not help but be astonished at the number of faces he recognized. There were very few that he could not recall seeing in Logan Station at one time or another. Most, he could call by name: Ed McClellan, the bookkeeper for the Southern Lumber Company, Buster Landers, soda jerk at The Owl Drug Store no less, Fred Oates, assistant manager of the Dixie Store, Rudy Hess, owner of Hess's Grocery, Marvin Singer, sometimes door-to-door salesman of crockery (and often out of work), Hi Graham, station master at the railroad depot, and on and on.

Buck let the commotion over being unmasked settle briefly. At last he quietly announced, "That's good, boys. It seems like a considerable improvement to me. I know most of you fellows. I reckon all of you know me. This Ku Klux business is craziness. It's no way to solve the problems here, or any other place. Get in your cars, get on your horses, and go home."

Disrobed, they stood indecisive. Buck caught covert glances as a few looked surreptitiously around at other members. There was the occasional mutter of low voiced conversational exchange. Buck thought they seemed like a bunch of small boys caught playing naked in the woods. Guilty, as if unsure what they ought to do, a few started drifting off down the hill, but it was still no mass exodus.

The Reverend Jellico stood off crying like a baby, still painfully squirming and severely conscious of the buckshot wounds in his back. Others began moving down the slope now, and Buck heard a motor start up. The meeting ground was emptying. It was obvious that the Exalted King of Knights was the most reluctant to go. Buck walked up to him.

"All right, Hull," he said dogmatically, "get the hell out of here!"

Hull tried to preserve his dignity with a show of huffiness, but it was too late now. He went toward Jellico, saying, "Come along, Reverend. There'll be another time," and he helped the Avenging Angel down the hill.

As the last of the Klansmen, reverted now to the commonplace clerks, bookkeepers, and wage earners that they were, climbed over the barbwire fence, Buck approached Wiley Lester and Ruby Pickard. Keeping a wary eye down the long reach of the slope, Buck said:

"Hang in close to me. Let's walk off into the timber as easy as we can. The less attention we attract the better. Some of that bunch may decide to come back."

Wiley Lester, touching the place on his back where the blacksnake had bit him, said, "I'm ready, Sheriff. After that Ku Klux Klan, your jail will seem like a mighty welcome and pleasant place."

Ruby Pickard, shaken and frightened, was biting her Cupid's bow lips. She seemed even prettier to Buck, minus the stage makeup and lipstick. "Hurry, Sheriff Mather," she said eagerly, "or I may be trying to climb into one of your pockets."

They made it to the cover of the encircling timber, and Buck led them back to the hidden and deserted Ford.

Kaahti was nowhere in sight. Buck stood with pursed lips trying to decide what to do next. The moon was waning. She could be lost out there in the dark someplace. *Start the motor,* he thought. *Maybe the noise will give her something to home in on.*

He set the throttle and the spark. Cocking the crank, he prepared to give it its first hard turn when a crashing through the underbrush alerted him. He quickly and quietly motioned Wiley and Ruby to the far side of the car. Lester hoisted the Winchester he had brought from the pile of ar- mament in front of the fiery cross and laid it across the hood, aimed toward the oncoming timber noise. Buck no- ticed that Wiley also had a pair of .45 six-shooters thrust in his belt.

"You're ready for any kind of a shootout, Lester," Buck suggested in a half whisper.

"No use being unprepared," Wiley assured him.

Buck wished he had picked up a couple more firearms himself. Ruby Pickard was empty-handed. She saw Buck's searching scrutiny and said forlornly, "I'm hopeless, Sheriff. We have one skit in the show where I'm supposed to shoot a cork out of a popgun. I can't even get that to go off half the time!"

The noisy advance through the woods kept coming, near- ing them relentlessly. Buck made out the outlines of two shadowy approaching figures but they were fully upon the Ford before he was able to be sure who it was. It was Bud Reed, prodding a prisoner before him.

"Godamighty, Bud," Buck cursed. "We come close to shooting you—"

Bud groused, "Another bullet hole, more or less, wouldn't make too much difference to me, Buck. This rifle butt got my shoulder to bleeding again during all the shooting. This here is the fellow you left tied up in the weeds down there by the fence. He says you took his Ku Klux clothes. What ought we to do with him?"

"Holy smoke," Buck admitted, nettled, "I forgot all about him. And I forgot to search him when I tied him up. Has he got a gun on him?"

"I took it."

"Turn him loose then. Whoa! Hold it!" The crashing through the brush came now from the other direction. Too loud to be Kaahti, Buck knew. He hastened to take up his defensive position behind the Ford once more, but Bud reassured him:

"That'll probably be Mr. Wells. He came to your house about the middle of the evening, Buck. He wanted to make sure you'd understood what he told you downtown there by lawyer Wooley's office. When I found out what he aimed to do—"

"What did he aim to do?" Buck interrupted querulously.

"He was carrying a Sharps buffalo gun as big as a piece of field artillery. Said he was coming out here to kill him a few Ku Klux and bust up this meeting. You wasn't there, of course, so I offered to come along with him. I wanted to try to talk him out of killing anybody—"

The intensity of Buck's stare stopped Bud in midsentence.

"You what?" Buck demanded, gaping.

"Well, Buck," Bud demurred, ducking his head in embarrassment. Reluctantly, he went on, "I think you've finally learned me that a killing is likely to make more problems than it does answers. I talked turkey to Mr. Wells all the way out here, about Hynote, an'—"

J. B. Wells came lurching out of the brush with the buffalo gun pointed at the spine of Jesse Renan, the same hardware store clerk who had harassed Kaahti, calling her "Buck Mather's squaw," the night of the Ku Klux Klan parade.

"This here," said Wells, "is the one they called the Knighthawk. Some hawk! I flushed him out of that clump of timber about halfway between the fiery cross and the barbwire fence. Tied him up and gagged him before I started shooting."

Renan's hood was missing. He still wore his white Klan robe.

"Take off your nightshirt, Renan," Buck said wearily. "Where's your mask?"

"I got it," Wells said. "It's what I used to gag him with." Wells heaved the wadded hood out of his hip pocket.

Buck took the Klan outfit and threw it on the floor of the back seat of the Ford. He began patting Renan down for weapons, and J. B. Wells said:

"He ain't got no gun neither. I took it, too."

Buck saw the pistol then, in the waistband of Wells' britches.

"Renan," Buck said sadly, "I've got the most powerful temptation to beat the very hell out of you, but I've been trying to persuade Bud here that the killing and rough stuff leads mainly to more killing and rough stuff. I think maybe I'm going to be able to restrain myself for maybe as much as two minutes before I set a bad example for Bud. Now if you can be plumb out of sight and in that much time . . ."

Jesse Renan was gone into the brush with a leap like a suddenly fleeing coyote. They listened to his diminishing footfalls until it was absolutely certain that he was headed for the fence row where the horses had been tied.

Then Buck said to Bud and J. B. Wells, "Gents, this is Miss Ruby Pickard, and Wiley—"

Lester was gone.

"Well, I'll be damned!" Buck swore.

Ruby lifted her shoulders. "He just walked off into the woods while you were talking with these men." She pointed. "He went that-a-way."

Buck stormed, "Hell's fire! Well, thunder and damnation, let him go. But if that tramp sneak thief ever pulls another holdup in this county I'll have his hide nailed to my barn door if it takes me—" He stopped short with a sudden surge of alarm bursting up through him. Cold sweat broke from every pore of his body as he, in that instant, realized that Kaahti was still out there, alone, somewhere in the night.

The soft call of a whippoorwill sounded in the brush not ten yards from where they were standing. With relief flooding through him as abruptly as the cold sweat had broken out on his body, Buck answered the call of the whippoorwill.

Kaahti came walking out of the scrub oaks, carrying the shotgun over her shoulder.

"Kaahti." Buck sensed the tone of chastisement incipient in his own voice, and Kaahti said:

"My husband, you are not about to try to teach a Kiowa girl how to deal with the enemy?"

Buck took the shotgun away, handed it to Bud, and folded her in his arms. "I sure as sin ain't! Not after what you done tonight. But if we don't get this car cranked up and headed out of here before some of that Klan bunch figures out that they've been snookered . . . they could come fogging back in here to get even. We may all of us be needing some lessons on how to deal with the enemy. Let's get going!"

He reached up under the Klan robe he was still wearing. Buck had removed the book he had picked up from the ground beside the fiery cross and had been carrying tucked inside his shirt. He handed the book to J. B. Wells. "Here, hang onto this," he told Wells. "It's the book that Jellico, who appears to have been the Klan secretary, was carrying. He lost it when Kaahti shot him. Seems like his backside full of buckshot made him forget all about it. It may have some information in it that will be useful."

Wells fingered the book and suggested, hesitantly, "Ain't there something else you're forgetting, Sheriff?"

Buck studied. "Not that I know of. What?"

"All them guns piled up there in front of that burnt out cross."

"Let 'em lay there and rust in the dew and the night air," Buck said. "It'd take us the better part of an hour to get out of here, drive over there, and load up. Any Ku Klux who come back after us are likely to come with whatever other guns they own or can borrow anyhow. Let's go."

They climbed in the Ford, Kaahti in front, Wells, Bud, and Ruby in back. Buck cranked, jumped in under the steering wheel, and began backing out for the trip into Logan Station. As they crept down the rough, stump filled trail toward the section line road, J. B. Wells kept lighting matches, reading the book he held in his lap.

"Great day, Sheriff," he said. "This book, as near as I can tell, lists every member of this Ku Klux Klan—by their right names. It's got the minutes of every one of their meetings. It even tells who went along on that first raid of Cimarron Bend. Listen to this, 'Brother Knight Roy Stribling, proprietor of the Floradora Billiard Parlor, accidentally shot and killed the brothel woman, Etta Redmond. We do not approve of Brother Stribling's business, but it is legitimate, and it is to his credit that, although accidentally, he has removed that woman of sin from our midst.' What do you think of that?"

Buck turned the Ford into the section line road. "Organizing that Klan was a damnfool thing to begin with. Anybody who'll do a stupid thing like that ain't likely to stop there. It was foolish to keep a written down list of the members, but not as foolish as joining up in the first place. Our Reverend Jellico, the Avenging Angel, is a methodical man. He wanted to be sure everybody got their names recorded in his good book so they could get their just rewards and recognition."

"I hope that you'll see that they do," Wells urged.

"Buck," Bud said speculatively, "I doubt we'll see any more of the Ku Klux, tonight or any other night. The more I think about it, the more it seems to me them fellows was pretty glad to get a chance to go home, instead of to jail."

"Our jail wouldn't have held them all," Buck said.

"Some of them may pack up and disappear for a while," Bud guessed, "hoping all this will just die down."

"It's not going to," Buck replied with hard resolution. "I'm going to take that book to the capital and turn it over to the territorial governor and the attorney general. I aim to file warrants, make arrests, and press for trials. I think the Territorial Peace Officers' Association will back me to a man. There ain't none of them wants a mess like this to deal with."

The Ford reached the end of the section line, and the main road into Logan Station. Buck waited patiently for a twelve mule team to pass. It was pulling a freight rig loaded with a pyramid of spudding casing, bound toward Cimarron Bend.

Buck pedaled the Ford into low gear, pulled out into the main road, and turned left toward Logan Station.

"Miss Pickard," Buck speculated, pondering, "I sure hope you'll pardon me if I'm wandering off where I've got no business, but I've been thinking you look mighty young for a show business lady. Seems to me I've been hearing of you around these oilfields for a mighty long time. How old are you?" he asked bluntly.

"I'm twenty-one," she said frankly. "My dad and mother are vaudeville people. I started performing when I was fourteen. Seven years does seem like a long time. Especially to me."

Bud Reed asked bashfully, "Do you like show business?"

"Sure," she said. In his rearview mirror, Buck could see the same characteristic lift of her shoulders that had emphasized her saying that she couldn't shoot a popgun.

Ruby smiled, "If I didn't like it, I'd quit."

Bud was eying her sidelong. "Will your show be playing somewhere tonight, Miss Pickard?" he asked.

"You bet," she assented.

"Even after all the trouble you had last night?" Bud marveled. "You must be worn out."

"The show has to go on," she assured him.

"Where?"

"In Oilton."

"Why that's only twenty miles from here," Bud said. Buck watched Bud in the rearview mirror. Deputy Bud Reed was up to something. Buck had known him too long.

"If I was to ride over there," Bud said graciously, "along about suppertime, could I take you out to eat?"

Ruby had turned, almost fully, examining Bud with a steady gaze. "An officer of the law, taking a show girl out to dine?"

"I'd consider it an honor, and a privilege." Bud's declaration was zealous and sincere.

"But you have a wounded shoulder," she protested.

"Miss Pickard," Bud said seriously, "I aim to eat supper tonight, even if I do have a wounded shoulder."

Ruby smiled, then laughed with gaiety, "In that case, mister deputy, I would consider it an honor and a pleasure."

The rhythm of the car's movement changed suddenly as it moved from the rutted dustiness of the dirt road onto the cobblestone brick paving of Logan Station's streets.

Buck felt Kaahti, beside him, breathe a sigh of relief. He glanced up at the morning star, glowing brightly above the horizon.

"It's a little early to be thinking about supper," he commented, "but it is durn near time for breakfast!"

Kaahti nodded comfortably. "Yes," she said. "Just drive on to our house, my husband. We can cook plenty of ham and eggs and biscuits for everybody."

XVI

The hour of breakfast, which had begun on a note of joyous celebration, soon dwindled toward a more subdued tone. They had been up all night, and with relaxation, came fatigue. J. B. Wells departed after a single cup of coffee, complaining that he was an old man, and his bones ached.

Bud left soon thereafter, remarking that he was headed for the Saddle Rock and some sleep. Kaahti put Ruby Pickard to bed in the spare room. Buck offered to help clean up the kitchen, but Kaahti said quietly:

"No, you should go to bed, too." She insisted, "You need rest worse than any of us. I'll wash these dishes when I wake up."

Buck shook his head. "I've got to get into town. There are a heap of things that need doing before I catch the noon train to the capital."

In spite of Kaahti's weariness, Buck would have sworn he saw a glimmering twinkle in her eyes. "You are going to file the charges?" she asked.

In hard-lipped silence, Buck nodded.

"May I go with you?" she asked.

Buck was sure he saw that twinkle now, and it puzzled him, but he shrugged.

"Sure," he said, "if you want to. The train leaves at twelve thirty-five. You can call a hack to take you to the depot, and I'll meet you there."

As Kaahti went on into their bedroom, Buck headed for the front door. He got as far as the parlor, where the leather

covered length of the horsehair stuffed couch looked inviting, and he succumbed to temptation.

He sat down, then lay down and propped his feet up,
thinking, *Danged if I ain't getting old myself. I'll just rest
here for a few minutes*—he thought, and was almost instantly asleep from sheer exhaustion.

He awoke with a start. Pulling out his pocket watch he
was shocked to see that two hours had escaped. His body
still stiff with fatigue, Buck stuffed his watch back in his
pocket and sat up. It was almost ten o'clock.

Two hours gone. Buck struggled off the couch and stood
up, his head swimming wearily. Walking back into the quiet
kitchen, he pumped cold water, dowsed his face and hair,
and finished off the bitter dregs of cold coffee from the pot
on the breakfast table.

Going to the barn, he set about the task of saddling
Chalky. By the time he had finished his blood seemed to
have begun to circulate a little and he felt almost human.
Riding toward town then, his thoughts turned grim and he
told himself with dismal foreboding, *The worst of this is still
ahead of me.*

The harshness of his feelings was further jarred by a
cheerful hail from the sidewalk, "Good morning, Sheriff!"

Buck glanced up to return the hail with the best grace
possible. It was Aaron Lully, the porter of Garland's Cigar
Factory, sweeping off the sidewalk in front of his proprietor's place of business.

"Good morning, Aaron," Buck saluted, recalling the incident soon after he had become sheriff in which a robber had
held up Garland's till late one afternoon when the porter
had been alone in the customers' room that fronted the
street.

As the holdup man had escaped, fleeing toward a corn
patch in the vacant lot across the street, the porter had
snatched a pistol from a desk drawer and fired a shot after

him. The robber disappeared in the corn patch. Everyone thought he had escaped.

But the next morning when the householder who was cultivating the vacant lot came to do some hoeing in his uptown garden, he had found the holdup man's body lying dead in the corn patch.

Buck had been hard put then to prevent a lynching, for Aaron Lully was black, and there were some in Logan Station so prejudiced that for a black man to kill any white man —even a thief in flight with his ill-gotten loot—was beyond the pale.

But Buck and Bud, with both the day- and night-shift jailers, all armed with scatter guns, had prevailed and Aaron Lully had been protected in jail until cigar maker Garland and his factory's lawyer had succeeded in getting the charges quashed.

As Buck approached the town square, he encountered more and more people who spoke to him, waved, or shouted a friendly greeting. It was almost as it once had been, in former times, when virtually everyone either was, or wanted to be his friend, and it sharpened Buck's curiosity.

Buck reined Chalky into the alleyway behind the Odeon vaudeville theater, then two doors down to the back entrance of the Logan Station *Leader's* printing plant and office. Behind the long building which housed Conrad Quinn's newspaper, Buck bowlined a single rein of Chalky's bridle to a downspout bracket above a nearly full water barrel.

Leaving Chalky drinking rain water from the barrel, Buck went through the double back doors. He made his way toward the front of the shop, past a busy job press, alongside the big flatbed press on which each day's newspaper was printed, through an atmosphere thick with the odor of printer's ink and the solvent used to clean the presses.

He reached the fonts and cases where a pair of typesetters rapidly slapped type into their hand-held rules while a third printer worked at page make-up on the stone beside them. Quinn's office was a littered cubbyhole just beyond the partition which separated the business side of the paper from the print shop.

Quinn, his back half-turned to his doorway, was hard at work fumbling through a tangled stack of ledger sheets in search of a particular one. Buck tossed the Klibe's book on Conrad Quinn's desk. It landed on the walnut desk top with a flat slap.

Quinn turned sharply. His rising glance touched the book, then met Buck's eyes. He grinned sardonically.

"So that's the indispensable document," he said.

Buck returned Quinn's stare blankly. "You mean you've already heard of it?" he asked.

Quinn smiled. "There's not much goes on in this town that doesn't reach my ears pretty quickly." He picked up the book and began turning through its pages, then looked up again to explain, "J. B. Wells was here waiting for me when I opened up this morning. Said he'd aimed to go home and to bed but his nerves were wired up too tight. He gave me quite an earful."

Quinn arose to thrust his head around the partition into the type shop. "Swiftly," he called, "set up in type the list of names in this book. Pull a couple galley proofs, then bring the book back to the sheriff. Sit down, Buck," Quinn invited.

Buck stood. "I'm taking the noon train to the capital," he said. "I intend to file a charge, and get a conviction, on every name in that book."

Quinn shook his head. "No, you won't!"

Buck stared at him. Having begun to feel that Quinn was swinging around to his side, Buck again felt doubtful. Apparently the publisher swung back and forth in this conflict like a pendulum.

Quinn stared back, looking Buck firmly in the eyes. He shook his head again and said, "You'll never do it."

Shifting a little uneasily in his chair, Quinn said, "Sheriff,

I understand you were involved in the Johnson County War, up in Wyoming."

Buck sat down. He suddenly began to suspect the direction in which the publisher was headed.

Quinn asked directly then, "Were any charges filed after that fracas was over?"

"There sure were," Buck said definitely. "Some of them against me," he added in frankness.

"How many of you were convicted?" Quinn pressed. "Was anybody ever found guilty of any of those charges?"

Buck kept silent, waiting.

Quinn went on. "I've done considerable checking on that fracas and I understand that when it simmered down, more than forty of you were confined under arrest at Fort Russell."

"Forty-four to be exact," Buck supplied.

"And that the authorities in Johnson County made repeated attempts to get you transferred to the Johnson County jurisdiction," Quinn said.

Buck nodded. "They finally did. We were remanded to jail in Laramie."

"But you didn't go to jail in Laramie. The judge there quartered you in the town hall. The same hall that had been headquarters for the cattlemen who were under arrest, and who had hired your gun."

Buck nodded.

"And that night the cattlemen threw a big party for all of you," Quinn continued relentlessly, "not as if you were prisoners under a charge of murder. It was more like a celebration, with champagne, as if you were heroes."

"Quinn, I'm not proud of any of that Johnson County business," Buck said, firm-lipped. "It's what made me so anti-mob, so against mob law, that I had to stand up against the Klan here."

Quinn kept on, "You received a change of venue to Cheyenne, where, again, you were not put in jail."

"Most of the cattlemen lived in Cheyenne," Buck said.

"They stayed in their homes. The rest of us stayed in hotels, waiting for the trial."

Quinn's eyes, fixed on Buck, were unyielding. "I have a newspaper friend, my informant in Wyoming, who went to Keefe's Hall, which had ostensibly been rented to confine all of you in Cheyenne. He went seeking an interview, and found the hall empty. Finally one man came wandering in. My newspaper friend asked him where the prisoners were. He replied, 'I'm the guard on duty here and I can't leave my post. If you want to talk to any of the prisoners you'll have to go wherever they are. I won't find them for you!'"

Buck shrugged. "There were aplenty of shenanigans, Quinn, legal and otherwise. But let me tell you something. Being under a criminal charge is mighty unsettling, in any circumstances."

"After some considerable time," Quinn said summarily, "when you were supposed to go to trial, the prosecution claimed that Johnson County was broke, couldn't pay the court costs, and that the judge had no choice but to admit you to bail, which he did. When the case finally, at long, long last, did come to trial, all of you hired gunslingers had just disappeared, having jumped your bail. It ended with all the charges being dropped. The order for your bail bond forfeiture was even rescinded."

"That's right," Buck agreed grimly, "but all that took months—during which I wondered if I'd ever get out of trouble—and during which Wyoming's folks built up a mighty strong resentment against the vigilantes in general, and us in particular. I wouldn't want to have to go back there, even now."

Quinn made his point pensively, "If every one of the cattlemen in that enforcer outfit had been found guilty, the way the folks on the other side thought they should, it would have broken the cattle business in Wyoming, just the same as if all these Ku Klux Klan members are charged and found guilty, it will break Logan Station. If you had been found guilty, you would have gone to jail for a long time, instead of winding up here with such a distaste for vigilante law and mob violence, and a sufficiently high set of ideals to break up this Ku Klux Klan."

"Are you trying to tell me I hadn't ought to file charges against any of these Klan members?" Buck asked.

Quinn shook his head. "You have to make your own decision on what you ought to do, Sheriff. I'm going to print that full list of Klan members, just like they came out of Jellico's book, in today's paper. When you get back from the capital, we'll print the names of the people you've filed charges against, and what those charges are. We print the news."

Buck's eyes were far focused, his mind a study. "Well," he said. "You've give me some things to think about," and he knew it would take some time for the conflicting issues Quinn had set twisting and turning in his head to settle and make sense.

"I think it is altogether unlikely," Quinn said, "that after we print these names in the paper, there will ever be another meeting of the Ku Klux Klan in Logan Station. They've been pulled out from under their bed sheets. Everyone knows who they are. Which is a different proposition than strutting around in a mask, feeling self-righteous, with the idea they can do whatever they want without anyone knowing who they were."

Buck found himself agreeing with that. "I want to turn it over in my mind," he admitted.

"Here's something else to think about," Quinn suggested. He reached in his desk and took out two holstered .45's, the sheriff's badge, and Bud Reed's badge. "You'll remember," Quinn reminded Buck, "that nothing whatever came out of that so-called arraignment hearing. Hull handed down no indictment. He never even formed any charges. Everything was just postponed.

"So you are still the sheriff, in the full power of your office. County Attorney Peebly and I went up to see Judge

Hull less than an hour ago. Marley is a determined young
fellow."

"I never figured that Marley Peebly was capable of being
determined," Buck temporized.

"Peebly is young and inexperienced," Quinn agreed, "but
he has a dogged determination to see the right carried out.
He's going to lose some battles in this life, like the one he
lost at your arraignment. But he's not going to lose any
wars."

"What did Judge Hull have to say?" Buck asked.

"He wasn't there." Quinn smiled. "We telephoned his
wife and she said he'd been called out of town."

Quinn shoved the guns and badges across the desk. "The
point is that, after last night, no one is going to have any
stomach for pressing any charges against you. Not Judge
Hull and especially not the Reverend Mark Jellico, who, by
the way, it seems has also been called out of town."

A printer's devil came into the office carrying the Klibe's
book and a pair of long galley proofs. "Swifty's finished,"
said the ink-stained young devil.

Quinn said, "Thank you, Eddie." He kept a galley proof,
handing the other and the book to Buck. "Take this galley
to the capital with you," he suggested. "It may come in
handy for ready reference."

Buck picked up his holstered .45 and took his time strap-
ping it on. He pinned on his badge. As he wrapped Bud's
cartridge belt around his deputy's revolver and pocketed the
other badge, Quinn concluded sardonically:

"Another piece of news I anticipate we'll be printing soon
will be the Territorial supreme court's appointment of a new
judge to replace Hull, and Jellico's church conference hiring a new preacher."

Buck gave Quinn a single, brusque nod, and left the office
without another word. He walked to the alleyway, mounted
Chalky, and rode to Talmadge's livery barn.

"I may be out of town for a few days," Buck told the

liveryman. "Be sure Chalky gets plenty to eat." He struck
out on foot then, headed for the square and the Saddle Rock
Hotel. It was nearing noon.

As he passed the Whitehouse Barbershop, Logan Station's
finest, Buck glanced in through the barbershop's window.
There, in the first chair, sat Bud. He was covered from the
neck down with a neatly pin-striped barber apron. The barber, a big, easygoing, and not overly intelligent fellow named
Duddley, who had been on the police force when Buck was
Logan Station's police chief, was shaving the back of Bud's
neck.

Buck turned and entered. Duddley paused to strop his
razor. Bud's hair was neatly trimmed, his face still ruddy
from its recent shave, and the sweet scent of lavish applica-
tions of tonic water flavored the air.

Bud grimaced sheepishly. "Getting all spruced and
spiffied up for my date tonight," he grinned.

Buck laid Bud's gun and badge in his lap on top of the
barber apron. "It looks like we're back in business, Bud," he
said.

Bud still grinned abstractedly, holding very still before the
barber's razor. "That's agreeable with me," he said.

Buck opened his mouth preparing to recount what had
happened in Quinn's office, but Bud interrupted:
"Say, Buck, Duddley here was with that Ku Klux bunch
last night. You remember seeing him?"

"To tell the truth, no," Buck said. "They was a big bunch
of 'em, thirty-some," he pulled Quinn's galley proof sheet
from his pocket and began running down its list of typeset
names. Sure enough, there it was: Bernard Duddley, barber.

The barber cleared his throat, sweating with embarrassment. "My wife kept after me to get off the police force,
Buck," he explained. "She said it was too dangerous, and I
ought to go back to barbering like I was when we first got
married. So I done it. But barbering gets awful boring and I
guess the Ku Klux Klan looked like a little excitement. I'm

sure sorry, Buck. I didn't aim to cause you and Bud all that trouble."

"Duddley says he's through with Ku Kluxing," Bud chuckled. "Ain't that right, Duddley?"

The barber plainly saw little humor in all this. "I sure am," he paused, shamefaced, to wipe the shaving lather from his razor. "I guess there ain't no way I can apologize, Buck," he said earnestly, "but I feel like hell. I ought to have pitched in with you out there last night as soon as I figured out who you were! But it caught me flat-footed. All it seemed like I could do was just stand there."

Bud said banteringly, "He went back out there this morning and got his rabbit hunting shotgun. Says most of the rest of the bunch had beat him there. Wasn't many guns left in the pile."

"But I don't believe a single one of the boys had picked up his white mask and robe," Duddley blurted eagerly. "Them hoods and robes was all piled up there in front of what was left of the fiery cross, just like we left 'em last night."

Buck grunted.

"I'm catching the train to the capital, Bud," he said. "I'm leaving you in charge here."

Bud's face fell drastically. "But, Buck," Bud appealed, crestfallen, "I was going to Oilton to take Ruby Pickard out to supper tonight!"

"Maybe I've got an alternate suggestion," Buck said.

While barber Duddley finished his work and put up his razor, removed the barber apron and shook it out on the floor, Buck went to the wall telephone. Bud sat glumly transfixed in the barber chair while Buck completed his call and returned to report:

"Kaahti was just about to leave the house. A hack is picking her up to bring her to the depot to meet me. She says she and Ruby Pickard just finished doing the dishes, and Ruby is in the bedroom fixing herself up. As soon as the hack drops Kaahti off at the depot it is supposed to go back to my house and get Ruby and carry her to Oilton to catch up with her show troupe.

"I told Kaahti not to send the hack back to our house, that there'd be some transportation out there for the pretty Miss Pickard and mighty soon. Now you hie yourself out to my house, crank up that Ford, drive Ruby Pickard out to Oilton, then get back to Cimarron Bend so you can keep a lid on things there tonight."

Bud was instantly out of the barber chair, strapped on his holstered gun, pinned on his badge and grabbed his hat to head for the door. He jerked open the barbershop door, then hauled up sharply and turned to face Buck.

"I don't know about this, Buck," he said doubtfully. "You know I've never drove a car but a time or two."

"Then you need the practice," Buck declared. "Get on your way!"

Buck walked on down to the depot, arriving there as Kaahti's hack came pulling up across the red brick cobblestones. He watched her step decorously down from the carriage, opening her purse and reaching up to pay the driver as the westbound daily local that would carry them on to the capital whistled for Cottonwood Creek crossing at the edge of town.

The hack driver tipped his cap to Kaahti in thanks for what Buck knew was a too generous tip, then backed his team to the curb to await the arrival of the train and the probable custom of the drummer or two who would need transportation to one of Logan Station's hostelries.

Buck walked up beside Kaahti as the approaching train's whistle howled woefully, entering the yard limits. Keeping the Klibe's record book locked beneath his upper arm, Buck relieved Kaahti of the straw suitcase and grip she carried. The train came on in, thundering past them as they stood together on the depot platform, unable to speak in the clamor of clanging bell and braking engine wheels as thrusting drivers felt the resistance of backing steam.

The roar of passing tender and mail-baggage car, the squeal of iron on iron as the parlor car and diner passed, slowing, then the final deafening hiss of steam released from driver cylinders down the line as the passenger coach ground to a halt before them.

The porter swung down out of the chair car to plant his iron stepping stool on the station platform and a scattering of passengers began descending. The Logan Station stop was a short one. Half a hundred yards down the track, Buck watched the engineer step down out of the cab and begin his circle tour of the engine, touching the driver cranks with his long spouted oil can.

The conductor was staring down at the railroad watch in his palm and shouting "All abo-o-o-ard—" as the last descending passenger stepped off the porter's stool. Buck handed Kaahti up into the chair car vestibule and, as the porter relieved him of the luggage, Buck asked, "Dinner still being served in the dining car?"

"Yas, sah!" the porter assured him. "Will be for a while yet."

"Fine," said Buck. "Just put those grips in the overhead rack. We'll be back pretty soon."

"Right, Sheriff Mather," the porter's smile attested his knowledge of Buck's record of resisting racial bigotry. "I'll have two good seats for you."

The train jerked in starting and it was Buck's turn to feel a twinge of guilt at proffering too big a tip. Carrying the Klibe's book, with Quinn's galley proofs folded inside the book's pages, Buck followed Kaahti along an increasingly unstable aisle as the locomotive gained speed in its out passage through the Logan Station freight yards.

Seated in the dining car, both perused the menus already open on the white tablecloth amid shining cutlery before them. It was now near one o'clock and they had the car almost to themselves with the last of the diners drifting out, leaving a lone drummer lingering over his coffee at the far end of the car.

The waiter came to take their orders, departed, and returned almost immediately with salad and dressing. Buck doctored up his green salad spicily with garlic and hot sauce, and said, with some reluctance:

"Kaahti, I've never told you a lot about my little foray up into Wyoming in '92."

Kaahti said gently, "You do not have to explain your past to me, my husband."

Buck took a ruminative bite, and spoke around it, "I reckon it's enough to say I went up there thinking I'd been hired by law abiding ranchers to put down a flood of cattle stealing the local law couldn't handle. Before it was over, I knew that while there was plenty of rustling and brand burning going on, it was mostly a fight between cattlemen and nesters who were filing homesteads on ranch land the big land holders didn't want to turn loose of."

"That has been clear from the parts of it you have told me," Kaahti said. "Especially about the killing of those two young cowboys—"

She hesitated and Buck filled in, "Nate Champion and Nick Ray."

They ate as they talked, and she studied him sympathetically. "That is the part that weighs heaviest on you," she said.

"It used to be," he agreed. "But now maybe it's the fact that none of us, the cattlemen, or us gunslingers they hired, ever rightly stood trial for those killings. Oh, there was plenty maneuvering in the courts, but it all petered out in postponements, changes of venue, and legal fumadiddle, and the charges were all finally dismissed."

The waiter came to remove the salad plates, replacing them with the small steaks Buck had ordered with Kaahti's approval.

Kaahti conjectured somberly, "And now that torments you as much as those other long ago wrongs that were committed."

The steaks were tender, succulent, delicious, but Buck was too perturbed to savor their goodness. "Particularly now that I'm on the law side of a mob action, in which a woman has been killed without cause, and other people hurt, along with plenty of property damage."

"And you fear the charges you go to the capital to file will come to naught," Kaahti guessed.

"Just like they did in Johnson County." Buck nodded. "Quinn even implies that I might as well not file my charges."

"But the fact that they are filed, that people do have to go to court, that it will take the Klan members a long time to get out of trouble, don't you think that will count for something?" Kaahti asked earnestly.

Buck pondered. "Yes, it surely will. I've got to file the charges and see it through."

The waiter paused to refill their coffee cups. Buck picked up Jellico's record book from where he had laid it on the table, removed the galley proof, and began writing on the back of it. *Caleb Hull—inciting to riot, Mark Jellico—assault with a deadly weapon, Roy Stribling—murder, Bruno Toombs—criminal assault, all Klan members—wanton destruction of property.*

"Those are the charges you will file?" Kaahti asked.

Buck handed her the list. "The Klan members will get together and hire the trickiest lawyer they can find."

"Who is Bruno Toombs?" she asked.

"I got his name out of Jellico's book," Buck said. "He's listed as the Klud. They must have slipped him from the Klan's national headquarters. Maybe he was sent here as an organizer. I never saw him before I shot him in the arm to keep him from laying that lash across Ruby Pickard's back. I anticipate he's long gone and we'll probably never see him again."

Kaahti put down the coffee she had been drinking. "Roy Stribling—murder," she said firmly. "That is good!"

"I'll file the charge in the first degree," Buck asserted. "It'll be reduced," he predicted. "I expect Roy will sell the Floradora and use the money to pay some slick eastern shyster to get him off altogether."

"It is hardly a pleasant prospect to lose everything you own, and end up with only disgrace," she countered.

"No," Buck said half-heartedly. "Anyway, Quinn insists the Klan is done for here, and I think that his publicity will help see to it that it is. Maybe someday we'll have courts that are effective in dealing with mobs." He stared out the train window across the prairie distance. "We sure don't have now."

"My husband," Kaahti encouraged him, "your honor has been redeemed, and you are restored to your authority." She reached across the table to take one of his hands in both of hers. "When I was a small girl it took my people many long journeys to gather the poles for a single tepee. Then there was the hunting and tanning of hides to make its covering—"

"I know"—Buck's voice rose with frustration—"I'm too impatient. Waiter! Where's our dessert?"

He grinned at her suddenly. "At least we've got a few hides tanned in this fracas. Maybe we can tan a few more."

She nodded enthusiastically. "You should do everything you can, which is what you are doing. Now stop worrying and punishing yourself."

The waiter brought two heaping dishes of assorted flavors of ice cream. "Fresh from Rushing's in Logan Station, Sheriff," he assured Buck. "We fast loaded it while we were stopped at the depot."

Buck sampled a bite of the strawberry. "Larrapin!" he assured the waiter with too hearty approbation, in apology for his shouted summons a few minutes ago.

"When we get to the capital," Buck told Kaahti, "we are going to stay in the best hotel in town. It'll be late when we get there this evening, and tomorrow's Saturday, a hard day to get much done, so I expect we'll have to stay over the weekend. We'll go to the Orpheum for the vaudeville, and to the Nickelodeon to see William S. Hart, or Wallace Reid and Lillian Gish—"

"With no Ku Klux Klan to creep in and surround us," she said, "to send us scooting off through the night over rough country, with you thinking up dangerous ways to get us in more terrible trouble."

"Nope," Buck asserted. "We're going to have a pleasant evening and an enjoyable weekend. When we get tired of the trivial delights of our wicked capital city tonight, we'll go back to our own quiet hotel room, and who knows—"